EXTINCTION ISLAND

catt dahman

To: Limmerfer, Ollie, TS, Murron, Finn, Procol, Baby Winnie, Limmerfer 1, Pickle, Aztec, Trixie, Prissy, Flea

Chapter 1: The Sea

"Bermuda Triangle all the way. We're in trouble."

"That's makes all of us feel better," Helen snapped at Stu. She wanted to slap him; actually, she had wanted to several times over the last few days, but that wouldn't fix his sour disposition.

He didn't acknowledge her response. He didn't care, and he didn't get it, anyway. All he cared about right now were the sky and sea. It was something he had never seen, and he found it fascinating, but spooky. He loved reading about sea anomalies, and he liked the chance to see one. He wanted to enjoy the eerie experience and at least pretend that he was in the middle of something other worldly.

Instead of the usual, bright blue sky, golden light, and wispy white clouds, there was a lot of yellow, black, and purple. The sky was a mass of bruises. The sky itself was a urine-yellow, but cloudy as if infected and full of poison. Rolling in were deep purple, almost black, boiling clouds that looked as thick and solid as a fungus; they looked ominous. The sea, no longer a pretty, clear turquoise, was dark and seemed to be covered in an oily yellow film, but that was only a reflection of the sky.

Even though the waves were growing, they were sluggish, twisting upon themselves and threatening. They no longer lapped at the boat but rolled it.

"Is it foggy out here?" Helen asked. The third person, standing with them, shook his head. "Not like regular fog. It's more like a haze. You see it in big cities, right? What causes this, Stu?"

"I don't know. How would I know?"

"You've been on your dad's yacht enough. Have you ever seen the sky look this way? Yellow?"

"No, never. It's got to be something weird: Bermuda Triangle stuff, I like it. Just think...."

"I don't like it," Helen admitted, "I don't want to think. I want it to go away."

"I told Tom this was a bad idea, but he was all for it," Stu said with a cocked eyebrow, implying that he meant more than he was saying. He wasn't happy with the entire trip. He had complained out loud for days, criticizing the guests and rolling his eyes often.

Tom had finished his Master's Degree, and for a gift, his dad allowed him to invite a huge crowd of his friends to join them on a week's vacation on the yacht. It was a generous gift that all the guests were pleased with. They had days of sunbathing, snorkeling, fishing, swimming, and relaxing.

Stu had several issues with the trip. First, he had been on this jaunt around the Bahamas several times and was irritated by those who were excited by the scenery. It was blue water and blue skies. No thrill. It got on his nerves to listen to all the visitors commenting on the nice weather. What did they expect to find? It was beautiful. So what?

His second problem was the guest list: did his brother make friends with every freak on campus? Why did he purposely diversify his friend-list? Tom must have searched the corners of the college to find people to fit each stereotype possible; they were all so expected. Stu forgot their names half the time, so he mentally considered them as: the slut, the gimp, the black guy, the Goth, the doper, and so on. Did Tom have any normal friends? Was he filling a *list* of typecasts?

Stu was bored with them. To him, they were losers that crowded the yacht; not that it was really crowded because the boat was huge, one of the biggest, so they had room enough to enjoy themselves, but it felt crowded with boring people. He walked over to watch the sky and speculate on an approaching storm, but Helen and Scott couldn't leave him alone; they followed like stupid ducklings and asked questions. Losers. He couldn't avoid them.

The boat was over three hundred feet long and forty-five feet abeam with five decks and a small pool. She had a steel hull and was fitted with an aluminum structure but then refitted with wooden decks and details so that while she was a sleek boat and huge, she was reminiscent of old sailing vessels.

From a distance, she was beautiful; up close the details were a little overdone and gaudy instead of being elegant. The teak wood made her a little weaker than the steel would have, but it was far more interesting.

Stu hardly cared. His father had the money to waste, and this was one of the latest ways of spending it. What was five hundred million for a boat? For all the area and luxury, Stu couldn't find a place to be alone to enjoy the weather; he was irritated beyond words at the others for ruining these moments.

"It's just a storm. I'm sure the captain knows what to do and would tell us if anything was wrong." Scott ran his hands over the railing, glad the boat was stronger than a storm. All the water made him feel faintly vulnerable. He hadn't felt that way before, but they had been fishing and swimming, but not watching a storm approach. There was a lot of water out there.

Stu snickered. "Really? He's paid to keep us calm. He wouldn't tell us anything was wrong. My dad pays a lot for the captain to say the right things."

"Gee, now I feel so much better," Helen remarked, "you're a spring of positivity."

Scott snickered and said, "Spring."

"It isn't my job to make you feel any way at all. We are technically at one edge of the Bermuda Triangle...."

"I thought that was the Bahamas," a voice said. The voice belonged to Joy, and she wandered over to watch the sky.

Stu ignored her. He was a good-looking young man, smart, and wealthy, and he saw no reason to pay attention to a woman who was like *she* was. He could do better, and she was beneath his notice. Joy was pretty in a vapid way: bleached blonde hair, big, perky, fake boobs, and bright blue eyes. She was obviously a slut, having made-out or slept with several of the men aboard the yacht. As loose as she was, she probably already had worked through the male and female crew as well. She was a flirt. Stu had her pegged.

"It is, but the edge of the Devil's Triangle is right here. But then, it's supposedly a million and a half square miles in size, and most of the downed planes and ships are outside of the Triangle anyway. It's a fairy tale," said Helen as she smiled at Joy's frown and told her, "It's just a storm. It may miss us anyway."

"That's what they all said right before they vanished," Stu said. "All those ships and planes…it's just a storm and pow…gone."

"I don't wanna vanish." Joy worried as she watched the yellow sky. She wasn't stupid and knew Stu was being mean and teasing her, but she didn't like how everything felt. She made her own observations, and she didn't believe in a so-called bad triangle of a dangerous area; she did believe in the storm and hated the way it looked.

"The captain says go below," Amanda called. She was one of the crew and one everyone liked. Not only was she smart and friendly, but she also took time to explain interesting parts of working on a yacht this size. She looked nice and neat in her uniform and had dark hair cut short and brushed carefully into a professional style. She was a fun member of the crew.

"Is anything wrong?" Scott asked. Unconsciously, he moved closer to the woman, protectively. "The sky looks strange."

"Nothing is wrong at all unless you want to get soaked, blown over the side, or hit by lightning," Amanda laughed. "The captain prefers to keep everyone safe, and that means being below. It's just a storm. Very normal. But it's not smart to be out in one, whether on land or sea. The crew can handle things." Men moved around the big boat, checking to be sure everything was tied down tightly.

"Is the color normal? Look at the sky. And the clouds are really black. It's hazy and creepy out here," Stu said, "I've never seen anything like this. We're right in the Triangle." He was excited and enjoyed watching the clouds roll in.

Amanda nodded and said, "We are there technically if you believe in that, but that isn't a reason to worry. How many planes and ships pass through here all the time and are fine? Laws of average, Stu. I've seen many weird-looking skies. The clouds and the storm are making it look worse. The cloud colors make everything look yellow. The haze is probably low level clouds coming in, but it looks pretty normal for a storm to me."

"She's paid to say that," said Stu as he smirked.

"No, I am paid to assist the captain, to keep everyone safe, and to be logical," Amanda snapped. She was crossing a line with her tone because he was the owner's son, but he was such a prick at times. He was trying to scare the others and show off, and it irritated her. He was always a little nasty to her since she had flatly refused his advances with polite, but clear words.

"Sure you are."

Amanda bit her tongue.

"Let's do what we've been asked to," Helen suggested. "Thanks, Amanda. I was nervous but feel better now. What is a little rain?"

"I understand. The clouds do look ominous, but this boat can handle it. And no, I am not paid to say that. Don't let old stories get to you, either. I've been in these waters often, as Stu has, and we're still here. We won't vanish." Amanda laughed as she led them to safety.

Below in the many rooms were groups everywhere because the yacht was full of Tom Jones' friends and family. It was so large that it could easily have accommodated twenty-eight people and almost that many crew.

Some of the guests complained about missing out on swimming or sunbathing, and some talked about the weather. They hated being inside when the day should have been beautiful. A few people played board games, and a few others sat at the bar, playing a drinking game. The concern about the storm made everyone either speak more softly or louder, but not in between. Normally, they spread out on the outer decks to relax or take in the sun, swim, snorkel, or splash in the small fresh water pool on the top deck. Sometimes they played billiards or rested in the movie room. Rarely did they wind up all together.

With the storm coming, they came together.

"What was that?"

Tom chuckled at the girl who replied, "It was a rolling wave. We'll likely get far worse, so be ready to run to the head...the bathroom...if you feel sick. We'll feel those from all over as the wind makes the water choppier."

"I thought I was over being sick." Wanda shuddered. She had spent a full day vomiting when they first boarded, but medication and peppermint tea finally had her able to walk around without getting sick.

"Nope." He gave her a one-armed hug. To his other side was his girlfriend, Kelly. "Wanda, I want you to talk me through when I get a tattoo next month. I hate needles, you know."

"Awe." Wanda grinned. She had a dozen tattoos and a half dozen piercings. "I need a new hole."

"You're running out of places," said Kelly as she teased her.

Wanda laughed and replied, "No way. There are places yet untouched." She wiggled her eyes brows.

"No way," said Kelly, cringing, "you are way too brave for me. Crazy girl." She liked all of Tom's friends, male and female. They were all so diverse and interesting to her. She had noticed Stu, Tom's brother, scowling at almost every one, but she didn't get that. All of Tom's friends were intelligent, funny or sweet, and he was missing out. The people that Tom chose had made the trip far more fun than when they were stuck with Tom's brother and his younger sister, spoiled and hateful. Tom's father was okay, his stepmother was dull and self-centered, and his younger brother, Vaughn, was the only other bright side when the rest weren't here. Even Tom felt that way. "Hey."

Kelly gripped Tom's arm. The roll of the boat made her stomach flip a little. That wave was pronounced, and it felt as if the boat stayed still a second before plunging into the next trough.

"It's okay. It's just a storm."

"In the Bermuda Triangle," Stu called. He always heard things that he could jump on. Ears like a bat.

"Knock it off, Stu."

"Just saying…."

"Well, don't say. We won't miss the comments at all. You're being an ass. If you want to be a jerk, then be so to your own friends; oh wait, you have none."

"You're so funny, Tom. It's not my fault if we're…."

"We know where we are. Let it go." Tom stopped the argument as Kelly grabbed his arm again. This time she dug in her long nails and made him wince. He wished he could calm her, but as long as the sea rolled wave after wave at them, there was little he could do. He noticed that the waves were closer together and deeper.

Chairs and loungers shifted as the crew worked to stow them in big stacks. They ran tight, springy ties around them to hold them steady.

"Listen to that wind," Wanda said, "it sounds like ghosts howling. I hate the sound. Thunder is more me."

"How Gothic," Stu said.

"And?" she shot back.

Tom was going to have a long talk with his brother and whip his ass if he had to. Enough was enough. For days, his brother had been rude to his friends, but Tom valued each one of them; that's why he invited them. Jealousy was not a pleasant thing to see.

Glasses slid down the bar, and a few baubles fell as the boat rose, paused, and fell with a shudder.

Like magic, Amanda appeared, and said, "I know it's rough, but we're fine. It's just a nasty storm, and the captain says we should be in it for a few hours. I'm sorry to tell you that part. It came up all at once and feels and sounds terrible, but it's not anything to worry about." She grabbed the wall as the yacht rolled again. She frowned a little. She was sure her information was correct, but it was getting worse, fast. As big as the yacht was, it was sure taking a beating. Little boats would have been swamped. She was thankful she wasn't with those out in the rain and wind.

Stu whistled a tune from a movie about a giant shark and made Amanda grit her teeth.

"We can't sink, right?" Wanda asked.

"Any boat can sink, but storms are common, and it would be a fluke if we did. I can't imagine that this storm could best the captain or the *Connie Louise*. This is a big, strong boat. It feels far worse than it is." Amanda wished the woman had not brought it up. "I've been in many storms, some far worse than this."

Glasses slid again, and a glass on a table fell off and broke. There were a few yelps of surprise. Before Amanda could smooth this over, a particularly violent wave made the boat shudder and tilt, causing a young man named Stanley to lose his balance and fall into a chair. Several flailed as they caught themselves. Outside, the wind was now a roar, far louder than it should have been. Metal groaned. The sound was daunting.

"The *Connie Louise* has a steel structure and is reinforced with teak, a very strong wood. The captain is working to get us away from this storm front. But remember, we are on one of the top thirty biggest, best luxury yachts in the world. We have a top crew."

Tom met Amanda's eyes. He knew it was a little worse than what she had thought. Her job right now was to be here and keep everyone calm while the rest of the crew helped the captain elsewhere. "Maybe we should put everything away that could fly around the room and hurt someone. Try to stay seated and relax as much as possible. If you walk around, you could fall."

"I'm a little scared," Kelly whispered to Tom.

He understood. The noise made it far worse.

Wanda nodded that she heard Tom, but she ran for the head to vomit, lurching sideways and grabbing walls to keep her balance.

"Helen, hand me a few lemon slices, will you? I'll go see if that will help settle Wanda's stomach," Kelly asked.

She took the slices and followed the other woman.

Tom was so proud of Kelly; she was scared but was thinking of helping someone else. She was a good nurse. She was getting an advance degree, and that was how Tom met her. She was smart, driven, and good hearted. He hoped that at the end of this trip on the last night, she would be surprised by his marriage proposal and would accept.

"Damn. Are you okay?" Tom saw two of his friends at the bar go sprawling. They sat on the floor, refusing to get back on the bar stools. Tyrese and Alex frowned from where they sat.

Amanda went over and picked up a phone that connected to the captain. She wanted an update. She listened and fought to keep from frowning. In this storm, how could the outside be any *more* yellow? Captain Worthington was tense, something which Amanda was not accustomed to. He said the barometer was plunging, the waves were getting worse, and the wind was ferocious. *It was all he could do to manage to keep them from flipping.* That unnerved her to hear those words.

A tingle of worry ran over her body.

"Have the passengers put on life vests, please."

She gulped. How would she do that and retain a calmness among the young passengers? She was about to earn her salary.

"Aye-Aye, sir."

"May I have your attention, please?" She steadied herself on another roll. "The captain said the storm is very strong. I would like for everyone to sit on the floor so you don't fall. That is my biggest worry. A fall could break a bone." She tried to deflect the concern. "Just sit on the floor, and lean against the chairs or sofas. I need for you to do this at once. I will also hand out life preservers. Please, put one on as soon as I hand it to you. It is simply protocol, and it's better to overdo the precautions than to regret not taking them." She smiled brightly.

Tom didn't ask, but he began helping Amanda. For some reason, he felt that they should hurry.

All the passengers had come into the main room and had frowns on their faces or were pale. They chattered softly with nervous energy. A swell made the boat tilt at a forty-five degree angle, and someone screamed. Voices rose in volume. Amanda looked at Tom; she felt helpless, and her eyes were full of concern.

"Bad?" Tom asked in a whisper.

She nodded.

They heard Tom's father, Durango Jones, talking on the phone with the captain. He was cursing and fuming, not that this was anyone's fault. It was random and a fluke.

Minutes passed.

Kelly put on her life vest and asked Wanda to sit with her and suck on the lemon. "I think the wind is dying down. The rolling isn't as bad."

She was correct. The rain had stopped, and the clouds were less threatening. The wind was easing up and was far lighter; it fact, it almost was just a strong breeze. The waves, with the water still dark, were farther apart and much smaller.

The crew and captain were grateful.

But Captain Worthington saw something to the east. It was a flicker and a lighter spot on the sea. He tried to determine what it was because it didn't make sense in the scenery. What was that? It was fast moving, dark, then light, and....

He blinked. He had been looking at it as something small and strange. It was strange, indeed, but it wasn't small. It was a tremendous wave, the last one of the storm, but the culmination of all the wind. He had never seen a wave of that size, and he knew with a sick feeling that it was way too late to turn the boat. This wave was from a different direction; it was a cross over, it was huge, and it was fast.

The captain blew the emergency horn and instinctively covered his face, despite his year of experience. The wave caught them sideways and flipped the big yacht like a toy, tossing it over and carrying it as the wave raced across the sea. The size and tonnage of the yacht didn't matter because nothing compared to the power of the ocean.

The passengers sat on the floor, most had their life vests on, but with no warning, the room rose and flipped, slinging all of them to the side briefly and then almost upside down. Bodies twisted and fell violently; everyone yelled or screamed, some in panic and some from pain.

Wood and metal cracked all around and made terrible noises. The shuddering didn't stop as they were carried along; the yacht was tearing apart, and sea water was rushing in, soaking everyone and horrifying each as he felt the boat sinking. Like rag dolls, they bounced and skittered around, slamming into one another.

They bounced across a small reef. Bones broke, and flesh was torn as the boat came apart. The water within the boat became red tinged.

The *Connie Louise* didn't sink; it just became a trash heap containing live people, and it didn't stop moving. It raced along with the rogue wave, never allowing anyone to recover as it was carried to a certain destination.

It was a long time until the horror stopped.

Chapter 2: Sand

Scott didn't think he had lost consciousness, but the time was fuzzy to him. In ways, it had all happened very fast, but at times, during the ordeal, time had been sluggish, like syrup. He wasn't sure if they had bounced around for a few minutes or hours. He lay in water, a reddish pool, and while it was shallow, it was irritating. Strangely, he felt the grit of sand mixed into the water, yet he was still inside the yacht. That wasn't a good sign.

Carefully, he rolled over and saw slivers of sunlight peeking through the wood and metal. That made him wonder if he had hit his head and was seeing things, but no, the sun was real and hot; the yacht had broken apart.

He was inside the same room as before, but it didn't look the same. He moved very slowly, waiting to find out if a particular place hurt, but he felt okay. Confused and achy, he felt no pain. He took inventory of his body and was shocked to find that while he was sore, had a few cuts and scrapes, a swollen and probably would-be-a-black eye, a nose that had bled but wasn't swollen, and a raw-scraped tailbone, he was really okay.

He saw a woman next to him, her dark long hair in her face. The hair was tangled and wet, and she stirred, so she wasn't dead;

Scott realized it was Helen. He hadn't known her before this trip, but he certainly had enjoyed her wit and intelligence on this trip, but to be honest, the second he spoke to her, he fell hard for her because in his eyes, she was beautiful.

He hadn't tried to kiss her and was waiting until after the trip to ask her out on a real date, but he found that they were always together, talking about deep subjects or diving off the lower deck to swim and have fun. He laughed a lot with Helen. He was shy, but he had to get past that now. Reaching his hand out, he touched her arm. Her other arm was cut and seeping a little blood, and he was worried.

"Helen?"

"Scott?" she asked in a whisper, "is it over?"

"Yeah, I think maybe we are on land. We wrecked."

"Are the ambulances here?"

Scott stopped to think. That was a smart question. Why had no one come yet? He was sure that there had been time and that someone had to have seen the massive wreckage of a yacht. Where was the help? The questions itched at his brain, bothering him. They were on a small island with limited emergency services. Sure.

"Not yet. It could be a while, so let's see your injuries and then everyone else's."

Helen sat up carefully as Scott helped her, and they checked her, finding only the one long cut. She said she felt sore, and a few bruises were already bluish, but she was mostly uninjured and thankful that she had been close to the big sofa that shielded her.

In the mess of wreckage, Scott saw the first aid box on the wall. They were right side up, and the floor was solid and even normal. The bottom must have torn away and tossed this section up onto the beach intact.

He refused to wait, so he cleaned her arm and made her hiss with the stinging of the antiseptic. He then applied antibiotic cream and bandaged her arm. "It's not bad. You won't need stitches, but the bandages will be irritating more than anything. It bled a lot because it was long, but it's very shallow."

He knew he was blithering, relieved that she was okay.

Throughout the maelstrom, Tom had held her, taking the blows to himself and protecting her.

Tom was on the sofa with Kelly where he had pulled her once they stopped moving. He popped his own shoulder back in place as Tom finished bandaging Helen's arm, and he made a slight yelp but then sighed as it felt better. It wasn't the first time that he had popped it back. The pain stopped at once, thankfully. He knew he was fortunate.

"You shouldn't use it for a while," Kelly warned Tom.

"I'll need it. Hand me the box." He did a fast first-aid treatment for a bad cut on Kelly's forehead that went up into her hairline. A small gash made her hair sticky with matted blood, but it was a scalp wound, one that tended to bleed heavily, but that was superficial.

She took the box and led the three to help the rest.

Wanda was near but twisted around a table; she was already black and blue with bruises, and her arm was mangled and mashed by something heavy that had rolled and fallen on it. She was out cold, but breathing steadily, and her heart beat was good.

Kelly huffed and said, "This looks very bad. See? It's broken in two places that I can see. But all this…this…her skin and flesh look as if they went through a meat grinder. I'm going to pour antiseptic on her, and she'll come awake, screaming. Calm her, Tom, and then find something that is supportive but has give and is soft such as those long noodle floats. If you can find one…no…maybe we can later. For now, use this or find clean cloth and wrap it, and then find something stiff and strong and gently put her arm in it, and tie it to her chest."

"Ummm. I. Kelly?"

"I have to leave you with her after I clean her arm because others need help. You can do it. If you see a towel…there…it's dry…keep her warm and calm. We don't want her to go into shock."

"Okay."

"I have to go to the rest; we have a ton of people on board."

Wanda did awake screaming, and it made others wiggle around in the wreckage. They could follow the sounds. Kelly shrugged and left Tom to be her assistant nurse. Later, she would stitch what she could if she had to. Someone should come soon and whisk them away to a clean and dry hospital.

Pamela popped up and called, "Help!"

They went to her. She had ended up rolling in the glass from the bar. On the positive side, the wounds were disinfected from broken alcohol bottles, and they smelled strongly, but she was covered in glass that stuck out all over her body. "Get them out. Please, get them out." She had removed several big pieces, but the little slivers were frightening to see.

"I can help. I'm just bruised and *hab busted doze*," Sue said. She let Kelly check her nose, and Kelly said it wasn't broken but had been twisted and bruised badly. She needed to leave it alone and not pick the clots out; she didn't need more bleeding.

"Remove the small pieces of glass, and slap a bandage over the wounds if they bleed much. Oozing is okay for now. Clean them. Here is an unbroken bottle of vodka and some gauze. Use it, but don't use all of it; we are going to need it later. Just give the wounds a swipe so they are clean, and if they are deep, clean more, but not so much that they bleed more. Does that made sense?" Kelly gave instructions.

"Got *ib*," Sue said.

"Don't move the big pieces, or she will bleed more. I will come back and stitch her."

"Is it my face?" Pamela asked.

"It's not bad," Kelly lied. The girl had been beautiful and had modeled some but never would again. The stitches she would need would be so extreme that they would destroy her good looks. She would look like Frankenstein's monster, but Kelly didn't know what else to do for her because the wounds gaped. If left alone, they were likely to get infected more easily and scar more. There were just a lot of cuts, and Pamela's face was solid red with blood.

"Kelly?" Helen sat back on her feet as she kneeled over who she was almost sure was Jordan. The body was big-bear-like and hairy like Jordan, and it was male; he had on one of Jordan's bright green and orange shoes, so it was a safe bet to assume that it was him.

One leg was bent but looked fine, but the other leg stuck outside the hole in the wreckage, a big hole that Helen could look through. Had he been anywhere else, he might have been fine, but this was one part that tore away, and the young man had taken a lot of damage to his body.

She saw sunshine, distant green trees, and sand, and she saw that Jordan's leg ended at his ankle. His shoe and foot were missing, and only white gristle, yellow fat, and blood remained. The bone shards were grey and stuck outside the hole.

Her head swam.

Scott put something to her mouth, and she drank. It was a plastic bottle half full of rum. Taking two sips, Helen willed the alcohol to calm her nerves. It worked; she stopped shaking.

Jordan's head was a pulpy mess since he had been tossed over and over, landing on his head and face. The ruined metal and wood had gouged and mashed his head. All over his face, muscles were showing and were stripped of flesh; deep black gashes still were trickling blood at a steady pace; and part of his lower jaw was ripped away, exposing his broken teeth.

"He's breathing."

Scott pulled Helen away, "No, he isn't."

"He is!"

"Helen, he's too badly injured. You have to let him go. He's unconscious. Do you want to work on him and wake him? He would suffer. Let's see whom we can save. Please, let him go."

She sobbed twice and nodded. She saw Scott's eyes were soft and wet; it was painful for him to make this choice.

Durango Jones, Tom's father, had been knocked out but was awake again and nauseated, disoriented, and dizzy. He wasn't sure where he was or what happened.

Scott and Helen gave him strict orders to stay where he was and rest until they returned. Kelly said Durango might have a concussion, but for sure he needed to stay seated. Knowing his expensive yacht was ruined and that his family and son's friends were injured or dead was enough to cause a mental shock as well.

"I...do I...."

"You sit here a little while and rest. Let's see how your head feels in a few minutes. You have several big lumps, and you've suffered a terrible shock. Please rest a little while." Kelly covered him with a mostly dry coverlet made of wool and would provide warmth, even if damp.

Amanda waved weakly for help, and they moved junk off of her until she was free and they could see how she was. She had a small but deep hole that looked as if she had been shot in her side, and blood steadily leaked. Luckily, the spot was where there might be muscle and fat, but not a major organ.

Kelly waved the other two away and stayed to stop the bleeding, clean the wound, and stitch the hole right then. It wasn't serious, but Amanda was missing two fingers that had been torn away. Despite being sea worn and strong, Amanda cried as she saw that her pinky and ring finger were stubs. Kelly didn't think it would help to tell her how lucky she was that they were clean, sharp amputations, and not mashed bits of bone left. Her opinion would not bring back those lost fingers.

Kelly had to clean and bandage those poor finger stubs. Amanda periodically vomited from the pain and terror. The others found towels and an afghan throw to use to bundle her up so she would remain warm.

"Thank you," Amanda said, tears in her eyes.

Helen smiled sadly. "I hate this for you. We'll be done soon."

They didn't see anyone else, so they climbed out of the wreckage and looked around, trying to discover what had happened and maybe find the rest of their friends. It was warm and sunny on the beach. Trash from their wreck had washed up on the beach.

There were no buildings, shacks, boats, or anything to indicate people lived nearby. The beach, other than having wreckage tossed on the sand, was pristine, making this feel more surreal. In one place was devastation and human suffering, and in the next was nothing but untouched beauty.

Scott ran to a body that lay in the water, rolling on the little waves that brought it up on the sand and then sucked it back to the deeper water. One leg was torn away but nowhere to be seen. The person was wearing a life jacket, but the missing leg indicated the cause of death.

"That's Hooter," Helen said. He was a crew member. She didn't like seeing another human tossed around like flotsam and jetsam.

They grabbed him and pulled him farther up onto the white silky sand. He was white except for his butt, the back of his shoulders, and one leg where blood had pooled. He was dead. Scott patted Helen's sun-warmed back. Three more crew members also bounced on the surf. They checked them, but they were dead.

Some bloody footprints were on the sand, trailing off toward the trees. There was a lot of blood as if someone injured had washed ashore and, despite injuries, had gone for help. Helen and Scott hurried after whoever it was. If the person were seriously injured, he needed medical attention, but whoever had walked up the beach was either brave enough to try to find help or confused by the nightmare and likely to harm himself farther down the beach.

"What the fff...hell?" Scott shouted. He ran, reaching for stones as he went. He lobbed the stones at the stupid lizards who were feeding on a body.

"Get away," Helen scream as she waved her arms and tossed rocks. It was ghastly seeing the buzzards and other loathsome creatures who ate the dead. They served a purpose, yes, but it is too soon to see this, and maybe the person wasn't dead.

The creatures ran away fast into the trees, except for the one Scott hit hard enough to kill.

Helen and Scott surmised this was Rob, another crew member, because he was dark skinned and was dressed in a uniform. It was difficult to be sure because his face had been eaten to the skull, and only bright, white teeth showed in the lipless mouth. His fingers and toes were gone, and the soft parts of his chest and belly were gone-- eaten.

"I think he was hurt badly and went this way in confusion and died. They were some type of carrion eaters."

Helen nodded and said, "Yuk." They went back to the beach, taking it all in. "What were those things?"

"Some weird lizards. Islands have weird things like that, I think. They were cowards." He wasn't impressed by them. They were no bigger than chickens and fat with muscles, they ran on their back legs, and were colored brightly: yellow, lime, and light green in mottled patterns. They might have been cute creatures, but like Helen, Scott felt they were no better than buzzards.

When they had time, he wanted to look at the dead one because he would swear it had tiny yellow feathers on its tail and shoulders. They were interesting animals which he was unfamiliar with.

Helen and Tom walked away and back to the water. Although the spiral staircase was bent and twisted and had to be used very carefully by turning sideways and sliding around, three decks still were intact and about 1400 square feet were on each.

Two other people lay slumped on the beach and looked up with surprise as Helen and Tom appeared. Connie Jones, with black streaks of make up on her cheeks, was crying and told them she thought her husband Durango was dead; he had drown. She didn't walk around to look for anyone. She stayed in her spot and sobbed. Emotionally and mentally, this was too much for her; back home she wasn't used to anything more troublesome than having to call a pool cleaner for a clogged filter.

Helen explained that Durango did have a head injury but was okay as far as they knew and was sitting still inside the remains of the boat. Connie cried more. Helen guessed that wasn't totally good news, after all. She was too shocked to make up lies.

"He's okay, I think. Kelly said Durango had to rest until his head was clear. He took a few hard blows, but he wasn't injured badly, other than that." Helen decided she was making it worse for Connie.

Connie nodded and watched the water as she picked at her cuticles.

Next to her was her stepdaughter Vera who rolled her eyes and said, "Can you believe this *shit*? Shipwrecked? Dad is going to have someone's ass over this."

"Language."

"You aren't my mother," Vera snapped. It was a usual response.

"That will be difficult to lay blame since it was a storm that caused it," Helen said.

Storms...they happen. No, someone made a mess, and look at it! Dad is going to be livid."

Helen shrugged and tried again. "I'm sure he'll see this was a terrible accident."

"I thought help would be here by now. I'm hungry," Vera announced.

"Are you injured?"

"My thigh." She showed them a gaping cut. It wasn't life threatening, but it was bad, and Helen was shocked that Vera was calm about it. There was no understanding fifteen-year-olds.

"Let's get it taken care of so you don't have an infection."

"I'll wait for the ambulances. They'll have drugs, so it doesn't hurt to fix me up."

Scott scowled and said, "I don't see any ambulances, I don't see buildings or people either, so we can assume it may be a while. I doubt you want an infection setting in, and it can within a short time. You need it cleaned and bandaged."

Vera howled and cursed as Helen cleaned it, and the girl tried to twist away and slapped at Helen until Scott took her hands and held them. Helen dried the skin as best she could, considering the blood still oozed, and she taped the wound closed. She wrapped it. "Kelly will have to stitch you."

"That crazy bitch is not touching me. I hate you! That hurt."

"She's your brother's girlfriend. That's pretty hateful. She's a nice person. And by the way, you didn't bother to ask, but Tom is fine."

Vera stared at Helen blankly with no interest. Then she said, "What's for pain. I hurt."

Helen reluctantly gave her two sips of the rum. Vera tried to yank away the bottle, but Helen was stronger and told her, "Be glad you got that!"

"Whatever."

Connie didn't say anything the entire time.

Helen knew that Vera was spoiled and not a very pleasant person, but even shock didn't excuse her bad behavior.

"Dude! Glad to see you." Davey ambled over from behind a section of the boat. He wasn't injured past bruises and a few cuts covered with bandages. With him was Tyrese who had a splinted and bandaged hand; thick gauze was wrapped around Tyrese's forearm, and he had cuts and bruises on his face that he ignored, saying he and Davey had cleaned them. The blood there was already becoming crusted.

Between them, Davey and Tyrese dragged Brian over as gently as they could. Normally, Brian used crutches and had a little feeling below his knees but still managed well. Because they hadn't found the crutches yet, they pulled him along the ground, and the pretty, white sand behind him was marked with a red trail of blood.

"Set him down," Scott directed.

"Here's an extra med kit. I'm not great with it. Like…yanno?"

"You did good, Davey," Tyrese said, "and you patched me. I thought you were as good as any nurse."

"How do you feel, Brian?" Helen asked.

"My feet hurt. Weird, I can hardly even feel them."

Helen examined them and wondered how both his feet had been crushed to mangled pulp. Anyone else would be screaming. It was a blessing in disguise. As far as Helen could tell, there was nothing that could be done; just like Jordan's mashed head was beyond her help, Brian's feet were too far gone. It made her sick. Brian was woozy but didn't complain, just groaned at times.

To the side, Connie vomited. "Can you do that some other place?" She stared with her face etched with disgust.

"You...."

Helen put a hand out to stop Scott. There was no use. "We're doing it here. I suggest you stay here with the group and rest so you don't bleed or cause yourself to go into shock, but you are free to go. Vera, you might bleed out, so think on that. We're all in a bad way, so try to be patient and calm."

Helen went back to looking over Brian. He had a deep stomach wound that she didn't dare clean, so she packed it with gauze and wrapped his injury. She didn't think he would live unless he went to a hospital. Davey and Tyrese watched Brian with deep concern. They had hoped help would be right there.

"We'll find some tee shirts to wrap your feet, Brian. I can't give you rum since you have a stomach wound, but Kelly will know more about that stuff."

"I'll just lie here and rest. I don't like rum anyway."

"I'll help you two, "Davey said, "like the vibes here are bad, yanno. I need a doobie, but I bet they all got wet."

"Druggie," Vera sneered.

Davey shrugged and said, "Oh, little rich girl, better that you call me only that when some others could call *you* far worse." He had a quiet, calming energy about him. Helen and Scott traded glances with Tyrese, wondering how Davey had done such a good job with first aid.

Stu Jones and his brother, Vaughn, stood close to the other wreckage. Neither looked very badly hurt. Stu pointed and said, "Beached whale."

"Dumb ass, that's Lisa." Helen was furious. They just looked and didn't try to help anyone. Vaughn, away from his brother, was a good kid, but he was scared and followed Stu's lead.

Helen ran down the beach a short ways. Lisa stirred but began crying hysterically at once. She was badly bruised, her jaw was greatly swollen, and the cuts and bruises in her hair were staining her almost curls red and pink. She was scraped all over and almost skinned in some places, but her cuts were not very deep. The salt water cleaned her injuries but also stung them. The guys helped her up, and they walked over to the rest.

She sat with her raw skin exposed to the sun.

Hearing someone crying for help, Helen, Scott, Davey, Stu, and Vaughn went to the other-but-very-twisted small part of the boat. There was a small hole to climb in or out, but only Scott went in. He said to wait while he checked it out.

He felt uncomfortable in the small, claustrophobic space, and he saw two men. Strangely, a small fire was burning out. "Hello?"

"We could not wait. Are the ambulances here? We need help."

Scott sighed. Same question. "No. There's no one. Yet. We've been giving first aid and trying to get everyone to one spot on the beach. We lost a few, and some are still missing. There doesn't seem to be anyone or anything near this place."

Fish nodded. He was a crew member and one they liked a lot, too. He was lively, but his almost musical, unusual way of speaking even now made them smile. "We have had some bad luck, but then some good luck because I was here for the captain. We are hurt, and yet we are alive. That is most lucky."

Scott knelt beside the captain. "Sir?"

"He has passed out, but his heart beat is slow and steady; he is breathing well. It is one of the better parts of this situation."

"He's so pale." Scott's shoes slipped on the floor. He touched the liquid that was so slippery and wasn't overly shocked to see that it was blood.

Fish cracked his knuckles. "We were mighty lucky. I have some broken wood and papers and other stuff to make a fine fire, you see? It was hot before."

"I can tell. It's hot in here."

"It kept him warm to prevent shock, and I needed it for the light and for the heat," Fish said as he nodded.

Scott realized Fish was without his shirt and belt. He asked, "Are you hurt?"

"Bruises and scrapes but nothing much. The captain was not so fortunate. His arm is lost, see?"

Scott looked. His arm...well, it was bandaged with Fish's shirt. A belt lay nearby. It was...wait; It was short, the arm was. Scott cocked his head, trying to understand.

"I had nothing but my brains and will power, a lighter and something to burn, and my wee wicked knife." Fish showed him a huge knife, eight inches long and razor sharp.

"I don't understand."

"His poor arm was caught under that metal over there and crushed. There was nothing left of it, but he was caught in a trap. He was bleeding to death, and I, well, I removed him from his crushed arm."

"You cut off his arm?"

"Oh, yes, I did. He passed out after a bit. I had this good fire and used my knife again and got it very hot in the coals, see? And then…." He made a motion. "I seared the blood vessels closed. The bleeding has almost stopped."

Scott blinked a few times. "You. He. His arm?"

"Above the elbow, yes."

"And with just that, and all alone. You did that?"

"What else could I do. I was indeed all alone, and I knew he would die. I did what had to be done. I used my head and thought what to do. You don't think I was wrong? Was I?"

"No, you're brave. I'm just shocked. I couldn't have done it."

"Oh, yes, you could do anything to save a life. You even could do it to yourself if pressed. People are far stronger than they think they are. You have some people out there crying over little cuts? The captain will not say a word about his pain. He is of strong stock."

"Fish, you, let me see," Scott said as he touched Fish's jaw and turned the man's head.

"Oh, my ear, you mean. It is gone: lost in this wreck, but I will be fine. Let's get him to a dry place on the beach as you said and make a nice fire. Someone will see it and come help, and in the meantime, we can be warm and dry and feel a bit better. Fires always cheer people."

Scott wasn't sure what to think. He had finished his degree to raise his credentials and was a history teacher. He didn't understand how these things worked: psychology and medicine. He was over whelmed, but he helped Fish raise Captain Worthington up so the others could carry him to the beach and start a fire. Fish gave the orders and took charge.

"Helloooo," a man called. It was Joe, the cook, and he was uninjured but tired because he had been swept farther down the beach. Picking a direction, he set out walking and found the rest. His face showed the relief at seeing other survivors. He happily took a few drinks of the rum and settled before the fire, watching over Captain Worthington and shaking his head at times.

Joy and Alex, down the beach in the other direction, saw the fire, smelled the smoke, and came to join them. Joy was so happy and upset, at the same time; she wept and kept her head against Alex, crying and shivering. "I thought everyone except us was dead and we were alone. I was so sad and scared."

"No, Joy, we are here. We are alive, and that is a very lucky thing," said Fish as he smiled and patted her foot.

"My jaw hurts. I mashed my lips; see how swollen they are and cut? I knocked out two teeth," Alex said.

Joy shared, "Not so lucky."

Fish shook his head and said, "No one had to cauterize your wound. You have both hands. You *are* lucky, dear."

Joy looked at the captain, shivered again, and said, "They were back teeth…like they broke off. It could have been the front."

"See? How lucky that was. I have a cut above my eye, but it could have been an eye I lost. My mouth hurts, and I bit my tongue, but I still have it. Loose teeth but all intact. Who needs an ear? I have the one!"

Joy smiled. Fish had a way to cheer people, it seemed. She was glad he was there. On the beach, she and Alex had seriously thought everyone was dead and that they were alone. Seeing others made them feel better, and Joy was glad someone was there to take charge.

Within an hour, the rest were brought out of the damp wreckage with Kelly leading. Kelly and Tom asked Stanley to help the injured because he seemed the most untouched of any. He said he was barely sore, but then he had been drunk, and some say *drunks fared well in car crashes, too.*

Strangely quiet, Durango hugged Connie and sat with her and his daughter. He had always been a loud, forceful man, almost a bully, but he was broken in spirit; whether from his head injuries or the wreck, no one knew. The survivors just knew that he had hardly spoken, and when he did, it was to say something like he wished help would arrive or that he was glad his family was safe. As the time passed, he spoke less and stared at the sea more.

Connie frowned often at him, wondering what the hell was wrong with him but guessed maybe his head ached and he was still confused. She missed her husband's strong, loud voice giving orders.

Kelly checked him again, shook her head, and said, "Concussion, at least. Without a hospital, I can't be sure, but his pupils are slightly off. Unfortunately, we'll have to watch and wait."

Two more of Tom's friends and some of the other crew members never came out of the wreckage, and everyone felt the crew had been carried away by the waves, drown, or something. No one could image why they didn't appear, alive or dead, on the beach like the others had when swept there by the waves. So many had been out in the storm, but when the rogue wave hit, they were lost over the side of the boat.

"They may be farther down one way or the other. We'll have to look later," Tom said.

Fish shook his head and answered, "The wave washed them away, over the railing and into the sea. Neptune claimed them. The captain and I would have drown except for the sea's mercy."

"I think we should go in and get everything useful we can find. Food, water, liquor, medical supplies, tarps, clothing, towels, sheets…anything…bowls even. We can dry most and then…." Tom said.

"I agree," Scott said, "I'll help head that project with you."

"My *brother*," Tom said as he smiled, "thank you."

Stu glowered. Scott wasn't his brother. Why did Tom say that?

"Rescuers should be here soon. Why bother?" Joy asked.

"They *should* be. They *would* be. So this tells me we washed up on one of the little uninhabited islands or on the backside of a small inhabited place. There are no people around, or they would be here," Fish said. "We are not fortunate in that way, I feel. We may be on our own a while, for all we know. It is best if we can be smart about that. Let's get everything out we can. Eh, Tom?"

Several of the shipwreck survivors joined in, and big piles of supplies began to form.

Kelly stitched flesh while the others scavenged, wondering if she would ever be finished. She was already down to using common thread for her work now. She felt that some of her patients might be all right, especially if someone came to help soon, but she knew that others she worked on had little chance of making it more than twenty-four hours. Brian's smashed feet and torn stomach, Captain

Worthington's severed arm, and Wanda's torn arm were the worst, but Vera's injury could go septic easily. The head injuries also worried her. They could have inner cranial bleeding, and others could be bleeding internally, for all she knew.

Kelly didn't have the supplies she needed, the help, or experience in this sort of triage. She needed clean gauze, more stitching material, a new needle, antiseptic cream, bandages, splints, and above all, antibiotics and painkillers. She felt as if she had been cheated.

"Twenty-three of us made it. That is lucky," Fish said.

Kelly wanted to add, *So far,* but didn't.

"Three dead. Many missing."

Scott spoke up, "Since it's getting dark, why don't we use the cooler temperatures to bury the ones who died? Rob was hurt and walked that way, and he died. We found these bastards chewing on him up there."

"Crab bastards? Sea gull bastards?" Fish asked.

"No, lizard bastards."

"They are too little to chew on a person," said Fish as he smiled.

Scott frowned and replied, "Not these. They're as big as a chicken or a rooster and walk on their back legs. And they have teeth and…."

Stu exploded, "And all of you bitch about *me* scaring people? In fact, I said it looked bad, and true enough, the storm *was* bad enough that we wrecked. Now, he goes on about big lizards, and no one says a *word*?"

"I was just about to say it is impossible. There are no such things," Fish countered, ignoring the fit.

"I saw them, too! Scott killed one with a rock. They are just like he said and colored yellow, bright green, and a darker green in some mottled pattern."

"Oh, unreal!" said Stu as he kicked sand.

Alex leaned forward and asked, "Anything else about them stand out?"

"I couldn't tell. I wanted to look again, but I think they had feathered tails and maybe tuffs of feathers or something on their shoulders or whatever that part of a lizard is called."

"Scott, you are a lying piece of shit. I was berated, and now you tell a ghost story around the fire, and everyone thinks it's cool. You said it was chicken-sized, but you called it a lizard, *lizard bastards*, I believe was the term, and now you retract, and say, oh maybe it had feathers. Wow."

"He didn't retract, Stu. He added. We both called it a lizard," Helen said.

"Stupid," and then he called her a very nasty word. Everyone cast him looks of disapproval for the word he used.

"Ok, *Stu bastard*," Helen replied, plenty mad.

He cursed again to himself and moved away from the rest to sit on the other side of Vera who also glared at the group. "This is my dad's trip. He is boss."

Durango Jones said nothing.

"I want to see. We can come back with torches and bury him, but let's go before it's dark," Alex said.

"Me, too," Sue said, "we Korean chicks *bees* good at science, yes. We wish to see bastard lizards." She spoke in a Korean accent, over-done, and made everyone laugh. Her messed up nose made her voice funnier.

Helen, Scott, Fish, Sue, and Alex left. They could still see the dried blood trail on the sand. Rob was still there, less shiny, some of the blood dried, but when the people came close, there was a flurry of yellow and green things, all legs and arms, running away. Sickeningly, the creatures had returned to his body and finished eating the middle section, throat, and face. They had started chewing on his arms and legs, the second or third choice of food.

"What, did you see those things?" Alex asked. The creatures were too fast, and it was close to dark, so he couldn't be sure what he saw. His heart raced.

"I saw, but...."

"This may be lucky if we can eat them or unlucky if they are not good to eat or hard to catch," Fish said in his usual ways of logic, "but these, I have never seen the likes of."

"Here is the dead one. They didn't eat him. Let's take it back to the fire to look at, but Alex...." Sue held the body of the dead creature.

"I *know*."

"Feathers. Good eye, Scott. Colors just as you said, Helen. Size right."

"Well, Sue. Did I make a mistake? Are they not lizards but rather some type of bird?"

"No."

"Okay, so I was right, and they are lizards and not birds," Scott said as he nodded, but Sue frowned. "What?"

"Still wrong," said Sue as she looked at Alex, "and I am one hundred percent sure. No doubt."

Alex grinned. "I know. Me, too. It is definitely one, well one of many."

"One what?" Helen asked.

"Compsognathes, or a micro compy if these are adults."

"I've never heard of *commasoathuses?* Huh?" Fish looked and sounded confused.

"Easy terms. It is one of the smallest dinosaurs to live that we know of," Sue said as she grinned, holding the carcass. There could have been much smaller ones. It's what we know, though, and it is definitely one. They look like lizards and chickens but are dinosaurs. *Living* dinosaurs, it seems."

"I thought dinosaurs died a million years ago."

"Sixty-five million years ago. Someone forgot to tell these guys that," added Alex as he shrugged.

"Then, I hope it's not like mice and rats and bats in the barn," Fish said sagely. "When you have one, you have the rest, so I hope that because these are here, the little dinos, that the rest are not…not the big ones. That would be unfortunate. Very."

Sue's jaw dropped as she looked at Alex.

What if?

Chapter Three: Night

"Why don't they come?"

"Shut up."

Helen sighed. She heard the same two lines every fifteen minutes. "Joy, no one knows we are here. We need to accept that. Please."

"Why doesn't someone *do* something?"

Amanda spoke, "I'm injured, but I'm not down for the count. Look, Helen is right. No one is coming, maybe not for a long time. Asking for help over and over isn't going to bring help. We have to face reality and do what we can. Stop asking, and do something positive. All of us have to do something."

"We have a nurse. We're doing well just because of that. We have a fire, and we're alive. I know this isn't what we expected, and I am sorry...." Tom's voice drifted away. He felt guilty, "but that is something we have done. We are trying, Joy, I promise."

"It isn't your fault," Helen said. She looked around their camp. They had plenty of water and soda, but that wouldn't last more than a few days; they were lucky to find that much. Joe, the ship's cook, had thrown together a dinner of assorted ingredients, but the galley's supplies had sunk, they thought, and food would be a problem soon. By the next day, everyone would be hungry.

Towels and sheets were drying all over the beach, so they had those, and they had found clothing that was drying, but not everyone had shoes, and few other shoes had been located. It was a crazy thing: they found a lot of some things and none of others. Cloth draped the wreckage, making it a terrible ghost.

Most of the injured were as comfortable as possible, but Brian was in poor condition and getting worse by the hour. Kelly said his stomach and bowels were perforated, so he was dying slowly, and he was becoming septic. She said his feet were so badly damaged that they needed to be removed, but he wouldn't survive what was required. She knew his blood pressure was far too low. No one knew what to say when Kelly reported that; it was a mild blessing that Brian was unconscious.

How Fish had cut off the captain's arm was something no one asked about, but everyone thought of. Kelly said the emergency procedure was perfect, considering the circumstances and added that she couldn't have done as well. They knew what he used and the general idea, but the sheer audacity and guts that the procedure took made everyone look at Fish with new respect. And maybe some fear. "How is he?" Helen asked her.

"Fish did a good job, you know. There is no sign of infection, and the bleeding is almost zero. I wish I could give him an IV to replace the blood loss, but he's strong and all right for now."

"Kelly, you need some rest."

Kelly smiled wanly and said, "I can't. I need more supplies. I need a clean place for these people. I feel helpless."

Tom shook his head at Helen and shrugged. He had seen the dark circles beneath Kelly's eyes, forming like bruises. She was exhausted mentally and physically, but she felt she had to watch every patient carefully although there was little she could do. "Kelly, without you, half of these people would be in critical condition. Please, relax."

"What was that?" Vera demanded. Her voice was above normal tone but slightly under a scream.

Tom turned to his younger sister and asked, "What?"

Vera pointed. She had been resting with her head in her dad's lap. He was very quiet and patted her face often, and she found that comforting.

As the rest of the survivors did things around the camp or sat and complained, she watched the tree line for no reason other than that she was tired of watching the ocean. She kept hoping that she would see help arriving. Instead, she saw something strange. What it was, defied her reasoning, and she wasn't overly-imaginative, so she didn't know what else to do besides ask the others if they saw it.

"There was a shadow up there. Some animal."

"Maybe it's help."

"It wasn't a person." Vera gritted her teeth as Kelly came to check her leg. It infuriated her that Kelly thought she was feverish and hallucinating; she wished she hadn't said anything. Lying there, she had to listen to Kelly mumbling while working. "That hurts!" She brushed Kelly's hands away.

"I don't mean it to hurt, Vera but I'm making sure it's clean and not infected. The stitches look good. You aren't bleeding anymore."

"Your stitches hurt. I can't believe anyone gave you a medical license."

"Knock it off, Vera. You're lucky Kelly is a nurse and could help, or you'd still be bleeding," Tom said. "If you aren't making it up or seeing things, what is it you saw?"

He had long ago washed his hands of his stepmother Connie and his sister Vera, deciding both were as shallow and selfish as any two people could be. Their snobby behavior irritated him. Stu was the same, and while he was Tom's full blood brother, Stu was as rude and vapid as Connie and Vera. Tom wondered if his own mother had somehow gotten Connie's children instead after he was born.

"I'm not making it up, you idiot. I saw a dark shape, and it moved fast up there." Vera was angry. Why did everyone always think she was being overly dramatic? "All of you are stupid and blind if you can't see the—whatevers--over there."

Stu berated her for scaring everyone, and there was a chatter that built; some were afraid, and others called it a cheap ploy for attention. Vera began wailing loudly, and arguments broke out.

"What do you think?" Tom asked Scott. He missed his mother right then and wished she were there to slap Stu and Vera for acting this way. Only Vaughn, the youngest brother, was helpful.

"I have no idea. She's your sister. Would she lie?"

Tom laughed, "Definitely, but she may have seen something. I don't know what to believe."

"Look," Alex called out. He had been watching the trees, wondering if there were anything moving around while the rest argued. He saw the shadow twice. On the third time, he pointed it out. "Vera is telling the truth, so everyone be quiet."

Whatever it was, it wasn't alone. Several shapes were moving around, and they were bigger than a man upright, but not something he could figure out. What moved like these shapes did? They darted and lumbered, staying at the edge of darkness and shadows so that they were not clearly observable.

"Are they people?" someone asked.

"No," Alex said, "not people. They are bigger than people." He stopped talking as a roar came from the trees and was followed by odd high-pitched barks and low whines. Alex always watched the nature shows on television, but he was blank when trying to figure out what would make those noises.

"Is it a leopard or a bear?"

"A bear on the beach?" Stu asked, "Joy, you are not very bright, huh?"

"Then, what is it? What makes that kind of noise?" she yelped as the roar echoed again.

Several reached for pieces of wood or metal bars that littered the beach. It was scary to hear the roar on an empty beach. In the dark.

"Be still," Alex warned, "I don't know...."

"Oh, shit," Tom said. He summarized what all of them were feeling and thinking.

The moon highlighted the top and back of the creature and showed a long tail. It wasn't a clear view, but it was enough to show all of them that whatever it was, it wasn't what they had expected in their wildest dreams. It could have been described as a large lizard or a skinned bird, but it was very large.

Around it, sand was flying as if a storm had appeared. It was impossible to see much as the sand obscured the view, jetting up as high as a dozen feet and around the area for several yards.

"That's where we buried Rob, Hooter, and Jordan," Scott said. In case anyone didn't make that connection, he wanted to remind them.

All around people covered their ears and cried out. The creatures were digging up the bodies, and the sounds they made were clear about what they were doing with the corpses. Bones snapped. A glutinous, wet smacking filled the night, and sounds like peeling off duct tape made it clear that something was up there in the shadows, feeding on the dead.

"Oh, hell, no," Tyrese said as he stood. He brandished a long section of metal.

Alex held out a hand and said, "Don't. Whatever they are, you don't want to go up there and get in the way of their feeding. They'll turn on you."

"But," Tyrese paused. He wanted to run over and beat them away from the bodies, but Alex made sense. Animals could be ferocious when eating, "what can we do?"

"Hope that there is enough food?" Stu asked with a smirk.

"You're an ass, Stu," Wanda said.

"You're a stupid Goth-whore. One-armed Wanda."

"That's it. I can't take your little snide remarks another second," said Wanda as she stood and ran down the beach to be alone. The animals scared her, but Stu's remarks were too much. She only went a little ways before she stopped. She heard a heavy thumping on the sand and froze, her instincts taking over.

"Wanda!" Tyrese called to her.

Her arm throbbed with severe pain that a little rum had not abated. She was dizzy with pain, blood loss, and the remnants of shock. *Be still*, Kelly had said, but Kelly wasn't as tired of hearing Stu's remarks. While she had lain wrapped in a sheet in a bed of sand, Stu had said things to her.

It was bad enough that sand irritated her as it crept in, that her torn arm ached, and that Kelly fussed over her, saying that there was worry of infection. Wanda knew her arm was far more ruined than stitches and cream could fix and that she needed real medical help as soon as possible. She knew that she was in serious danger. More than that, Wanda knew that she couldn't stand the pain much longer and was at the point of just screaming and crying.

Her last straw was when Stu asked her how she was going to work, being one-armed in her Goth-look. Before that, he waxed on and on about how Fish removed the captain's arm, making Wanda cringe with fear.

She stopped in her tracks, feeling she was being watched before she even heard the thrum of heavy footfalls beside her. She smelled a terrible odor; it reminded her of when she was young and had a pet turtle. When his water was very dirty, it had a vicious reptilian scent that was like body odor, but more pungent and dirtier. Over that was a layer of scent that was reminiscent of rotting meat and fish. The smell alone terrified her.

"Wanda, don't move."

She didn't. She couldn't unless she fell to her knees. She was making a keening noise that she couldn't stop.

"Be quiet," Tyrese told her. He stood close with Tom, Scott, Fish, and Alex. The others held make-shift weapons, except for Alex, who stared with his jaw hanging open.

"Tyrese...." Wanda wanted him to save her. In the moonlight, he looked like a super hero, an avenging angel ready to do battle, or a huge wrestler. Tom was strong, and so were the rest. They could help her. *She needed them to save her, now,* she thought.

"I don't...okay, stand straight up, and try to look bigger," Alex said.

"How can she?" Scott asked. He advanced.

In the moonlight, the purple hues of the skin were pinkish yellow; the flesh was pebbled and thick. The beast stood a little more than seven feet tall, was ropey with heavy muscles, and moved with stingy, compact motions. That was an illusion that it was slow because if and when it attacked, it would be a blur of action. It was perfectly designed to work in the shadows of the night where it could hunt in an almost elegant way.

The cadavers the creatures dug up were easy food, but they didn't mind fighting for living flesh either. The beast sniffed Wanda, figuring out what kind of a threat she might be. It smelled blood and terror. The other figures didn't concern it. It wanted food.

Some might say it was lizard-like, and it was, yet it was far more than that. That was the general shape, but paleontologists had their research wrong. Troodon wasn't a skinny little version of the *saurus* group. It was very muscular and heavy, not fat, but solidly built. His tail balanced him, but it wasn't a long tapering whip; it was extremely thick at the base and shorter than the fossils indicated.

Its fore legs were not short but were long enough that it could easily walk on all fours, but the fore legs were used as hands that had nimble fingers, ending in sharp, thick claws, long and deadly. Its big, fat back feet were enormous and sturdy and had smaller, but equally as thick and sharp, claws.

Alex was scared but also fascinated by this creature and thought it was the equivalent of a defensive tackle on a football team. He had never imagined troodons could be this formidable, but he knew that was what it was. It looked different from what people drew to illustrate them, but some things, Alex just knew.

Wanda went silent as she stared at the animal.

The creature sniffed, snorted, and cocked his head.

The head was elongated as expected; the skull research was correct. It had a very expressive set of eyes that shifted with every sound it heard. It sniffed at the human and showed a set of impressive teeth, something unexpected since his kind didn't get this big of a set of teeth until they were older adults.

Alex understood that fossils hadn't done this thing justice. How would anyone know that the bones found were the young troodons? Alex almost smiled, knowing this would change everything paleontologists believed. It was the find of a life time if he survived.

"Wanda, slowly step backwards away from him."

"Uh huh," she whispered. Her head swam with dizzying pain. She wanted to run but was too woozy to do that.

"Be ready. If he is alone, he'll let her go, I think. I dunno. All we know about dinosaurs is blown. They're nothing like...." Alex muttered as he thought.

"Dino...what?" Tom said, "no way."

In a rush, heavy footfalls surrounded them, and another three troodons appeared next to the first. They were curious but had already learned that humans were tasty. Dead ones. It was possible that live ones were even better. Yet they hesitated because as bright as they were, they knew that some creatures were dangerous even if these only smelled like fear.

"Alex?"

"I have nothing."

"Try."

"Back away; look big. We can either try to show force and risk making them angry and aggressive, or we stay back and make them think we are weak and are prey. Neither is a good choice, guys."

With no warning, the first troodon snaked its head forward and clamped onto Wanda's bandaged arm. Simultaneously, as was its nature, it grabbed her with its dexterous, clawed hands.

Wanda screamed. The choice was made.

People, back in the camp who watched, also screamed and grabbed sticks or hid behind others. A few covered their eyes or ears. They knew what was coming.

The pain was so overwhelming that Wanda's body collapsed limply as she screamed over and over, but the troodon was strong enough to hold her up in place with its hands and teeth. It just clamped down harder.

Scott and Fish tried to hit the animal, but the other three hissed and snapped at them. Attacking, Tom and Tyrese advanced. They managed to land only a few blows as they dodged claws and teeth; those hits only angered the creatures instead of hurting them. In seconds, the animals learned to avoid the weapons aimed at them and advanced quickly. Tyrese fell as one nipped his head, barely missing getting a grip that would have crushed his skull if he had been allowed to chomp down with full force.

Alex helped Tyrese to his feet and waved his arms, trying to distract the troodons.

Wanda's arm tore away with a meaty, wet sound that sent blood jetting. If she had been in pain before, this surpassed it because her nerves didn't go numb with shock. She felt each nerve ending as it shrieked. She fell and rolled, unable to do anything but lie on the sand and scream.

The men fought back, but the four animals aggressively backed them away from Wanda, protecting their prey. Her screams excited them. While three nipped and slashed, the first troodon clawed into Wanda's neck as it was accustomed; it was how to kill food.

Tom jerked away as a claw raked his arm, causing blood to pour.

"We have to back out," said Alex as he pulled Tom back.

"Wanda…." Scott dodged another lunge from the beasts. Had the troodons known their prey better, (and they did now, too late for a real attack, but they would learn from this), they would have attacked fully and killed all of the men. For now, a few of the blows from the weapons hurt when they landed on sensitive snouts, and one blinked and backed out of the fight as Fish battered its eye.

In the future, the troodons would know not to parry, but to attack swiftly and take out the food fast. Most food wasn't this smart.

This fight was over, and it was time to retreat and consider what they had learned about the new food on the island. However, they would take their kill.

In the blood-soaked sand, Wanda grew cold as time slowed for her. She felt relief from the heat of the night and shivered. It was not bad. She faintly knew that her injury had vanished because her arm was fully gone. This was a very terrible thing: her arm being one. Her pain was drifting away as her head became more muddled; for that, she was thankful, but she was far too tired to get up. The fight around her was terrifying, but the sounds, the roars, and snapping of jaws seemed far away.

Wanda wasn't sure why no one was helping her, and that made her sad. Tears fell, and she felt very alone. She always had felt a little alone until Tom and his friends took her under their wings and made her feel a part of a group. Tom was sweet to have invited her on this trip even if the trip had gone bad.

It was bad enough to be severely injured in a ship wreck and land on an island where there were no people and no help, but what were the chances of being attacked by dinosaurs? That's what they were, she knew. It was obvious. Wanda smiled a little at that. To see extinct animals was amazing.

She didn't hear them anymore and could barely see them as her vision became so poor that she only saw a small circle of activity. There was really no pain. She didn't feel the wetness at her shoulder and throat anymore.

Wanda's heart stopped.

Just as she died, two troodons grabbed her body and ran back into the trees, carrying her. With the three bodies they had found and then this one, there was enough meat for the pack. The little ones in the nests would be satisfied tonight, unlike most nights, and would sleep well.

Scott sank to his knees. He was relieved to see the four beasts run away, but they took Wanda with them; how could they do that?

She was just…gone. The beach in the moonlight was stained with sprays and patches of maroon blood, but that was all. Wanda was gone, and there was no way to get her back. He was sure she had died because of the way her body flopped and hung limply.

Scott felt relief mix with guilt and horror. And fear. He was full of emotions as he tried to make sense of what had just happened to Wanda. It was almost more than he could believe.

"They took her," Tom said. He knew they knew that, but he had to say it. Behind them, others were crying or shaking with fear as they held weapons. "Let go back. We can't do a damned thing now." He didn't want to leave Kelly alone over there. His worst fear was that they would come after her.

"You had no chance, Dude," Davey said. He had positioned himself to protect those who were injured.

Tom nodded and let Kelly scrub his gash. She was worried about infection and so dug the cloth into the wound and worked in the vodka she was using to cleanse. Tom gritted his teeth and let her work. He was glad to see how Davey and his younger brother, Vaughn, and several others had grabbed weapons and stood guard. Even Stu had stood beside Connie, Vera and their dad Durango, ready to fight.

"Help me understand, Alex and Sue?" Tom asked.

"They smelled blood and came as a pack. I assure you those are really dinosaurs. I can't explain it, but there is no doubt. Those kinds hunt in packs, and if we had pushed the battle, all of us would have died."

"I can't believe what I saw, Alex," Sue said. She was scared but also excited and curious about the creatures. "Those were troodons, right?" she asked.

"I think so. They are a little different than what we have seen and have learned about. They're bigger and stronger, but yeah, troodons. I am sure of that. Troodons times ten, though."

"What are you talking about?" Helen asked.

Alex took a deep breath. "I don't know where we are or how it's possible, but the first critters are compsognathus. No doubt at all. Those mean sons of bitches we just fought with are troodons. All of you've heard of velociraptors from movies, right? Well, these are like cousins to them. They don't have the back claws like sickles, but they are smarter versions, hunt in packs, and are bigger and…and more lethal than what people have always thought."

"You're back to dinosaurs?" Stu asked. He wasn't being sarcastic but was still skeptical. He didn't know what to think except that never had he seen anything like those animals.

"You saw them and what they did, the same as I did. If you have a better explanation, lay it on me," Alex suggested.

"How is it possible? We didn't scoot through a time warp, right? Did we?"

"No, Stu, I don't think that's it. With so many islands all over the place, we may be on a very small one that never really evolved. Look at Australia. They have weird animals that no one has ever seen except for there. It makes sense that there are places like this that have animals we aren't used to."

"If people lived here, we'd have heard of these things. It wouldn't be a secret, so I think it makes sense that we're on a small island and that we're alone. That explains why no one came to rescue us," Helen said. It really hit her, the nagging fear that they were alone.

"There's no help coming? At all?" asked Vera as she cried, "what now? What are we going to do?" Durango Jones absently stroked her hair; she didn't calm down. He could pat her forever, and she would never forget watching the Gothic girl being attacked and dragged away. Her brother Tom had been hurt, trying to fight the creatures; she would always have nightmares about that. Had Stu not been there, weapon in hand, she would have screamed herself hoarse.

"We make do and find a way to survive and get rescued, or we find a way to get back to sea. We stick together," Tom said. It was something his father would have said, much louder and much stronger, but his father was not doing well with his head wounds. "It's probable that people are searching for us right now, and when we're found, they'll find the creatures here." He couldn't say *dinosaur* just yet.

"Are you sure they're looking for us?" Vera asked.

"Of course. We didn't vanish. They'll know we're lost, so then they will find wreckage signs and then us, right here. Vera, they can name a creature after you…a Verasaur."

She smiled.

"We have some seriously injured people, Tom," said Kelly as she bit her bottom lip while she added some rum and wrapped it in a bandage, wondering when the wounds would stop. All she did was stitch and clean, and she felt helpless.

Then in the daylight, we search again for supplies. We can dive in the shallows and see if things sank. We can search the beach, gather things, explore, and figure out how big this place is, as we tend to the injured and avoid the monsters, and we will do it together. Before, we half-assed gathered supplies, but tomorrow, it's for real. We need everything we can find, no matter what it is, Tom thought aloud.

"And we need fresh water, food, and shelter," Scott said. "We can clear out that one part of the boat and make it a shelter. It isn't the best, but it's strong, and the way it is sitting will ensure that we can guard the entrance. It's huge, but the hole isn't that large. We will have plenty of room, but I think the top deck is weak and shouldn't be trusted."

Tom thought about that, and Fish said maybe they should move the injured there now and clear it out in the morning. If they didn't do something, no one would sleep at all. He cocked his head at Kelly.

Kelly wavered on her feet with exhaustion.

It took hours, but they moved everyone inside or directly outside next to the big wreckage. Kelly, like some of the rest, fell asleep a few hours before sunrise because they couldn't fight the tiredness any longer. Her sick bay was the bottom deck. The second deck was a place for the rest to sleep.

It was the longest night any of them had ever known.

Chapter 4: Day Two

Scott dozed off and on, always trying to be sure someone was watching the trees, but no other animals came to torment them, and when the sun rose, they stayed where they were, letting everyone sleep as much as possible.

Because of the episode the night before, they faced a problem when Brian died midmorning. If they buried him, they not only would attract animals, but would also let his body be eaten, something that made them sick. Fish came to the rescue as he showed them how to wrap Brian in a sheet with rocks and anything else heavy they could find and then bind him like a mummy. wearing their life jackets, Scott and he swam out as far as they could and let the body sink beneath the waves.

Everyone watched silently.

"That was the right thing to do," Helen said, "and I feel better about a burial at sea. I hope it's the last."

"We can only hope for luck. Kelly says the captain is doing well, and he awoke for a while and drank a lot of water. I have faith he will be okay," Fish said.

"Vera worries me as well as Durango and the captain. For all I know, any of us could get an infection and die. We have to face that," she said.

"That is true, Helen, but we have made it so far. My ear... meh...it will not grow back, right? But it is only an ear. I feel fortunate." Fish sat and carefully made spears and pikes from the junk they found. Wood, if long and sturdy, was sharpened into a spear. A sharp bit of metal tied to a longer piece made a lethal club that could cut and slice. In their extensive searches right off the beach in three feet of water, they found a sprawling spill from the galley, which provided cans of food, knives, cups, and pots.

Somehow, the contents had spilled before the galley section broke into pieces. The sea had been random about whom it took and how it broke apart the boat. Big sections must have sunk because most of the boat was nowhere to be seen. Fish told them stories of other wrecks he had learned about and explained how fickle the sea could be; it was unpredictable.

"You hear the stories and wonder. You think some of the stories about wrecks and creatures are impossible, but we have explored very little of the world's oceans, and there is far more we have never seen and can not imagine than what we do know. Once, it was said there could not be giant squid, but there are giants that we have seen and photographed. We see hurricanes, but no one can predict what they will truly do."

"But dinosaurs aren't part of the sea," Alex mused.

"No, but this island is in the big, blue sea. It's a mere dot of land. Mysteries are all over."

Joe, the cook, ignored all that talk and shifted his views quickly, trying to figure out how to cook a big meal on the fire. He knew stew and soups would make the food go the farthest, and he had enough canned meat and vegetables to keep them full for a few days, provided they found fresh water. The rest could worry about animals and mysteries, but he had people to feed. He had to provide full bellies and nutrition, things he was good at. It gave him a renewed sense of purpose, and he was elated.

But no one asked a cook's opinion. Had anyone asked Joe, he wouldn't have waxed on about sea stories, like Fish who made him smile. He would have pointed out that Fish's role was to amuse, lead, and be strong. Each person had a role even if he didn't understand it or wasn't ready to embrace it, yet. Tom was a leader. Whether Scott was a leader, he didn't know. Tyrese was a leader, too. And they worked as a team.

Kelly was a nurse, but few had taken note that Davey hid his smarts well but was also good at medical stuff. It made Joe smile to think people had missed that. The group was mourning for themselves and others, but they would find their strengths, just as Joe knew his (he knew long ago), and they would come around.

Joe was very glad to have the supplies he needed. He could have made do, but this was better. A full belly of warm food tended to sooth fears and put nerves to rest. That was why he was proud of what his job was; he was able to help the frightened survivors and give them some succor.

Once the searchers broke into the other areas of the battered boat on the upper deck, they found a compartment with fishing equipment and snorkeling gear. They could have fresh fish. There were nets and small crab traps, and all were in excellent shape, unlike the humans. At some level, they understood that the find would cover two areas. First, it would give them purpose, as well as giving some of them a job. Joe would have understood that well and would have agreed. The fresh food would be healthy for them and would help Joe do his job in providing for them.

Joe didn't need a degree in human behavior to know all this; he had lived long and learned.

Kelly was thrilled when they found the main medical supplies from the mini-sick bay. She had antibiotics, more bandages, real disinfectant, all kinds of creams, and pills. As some luggage was found, people added personal items so Kelly had several pairs of tweezers and scissors, and magnifying glasses so she could see better as she worked. It was better than Christmas for her.

Davey slid next to her with a box he held close and slid it into her hand. "My stash, like it's good shit. I kept a couple, but you can use this for...yanno...like pain and shit help?"

"Davey, most would have *bogarted* this. You are a really good hearted guy. You are amazing. It will help tremendously with the pain."

"I thought Vera was a little bitch mostly, but she's alone right now, and like maybe she will smoke one with me? I can talk her into it, play on her bad-girl side if you say it's okay."

"It *is* okay. I never would have advocated it, but that child needs relief something awful. She's just a kid, a whiney one and rude, but a scared kind, and her daddy is hurt. See if she'll sleep all afternoon, too. It will help her more than anything I have, and she'll be out of the pain for a few hours. Sleep can heal as well as many things can."

"Gotcha, Nurse Kelly, hey."

Kelly turned back.

"Tom did good. Like he picked a winner in you."

"He picked a winner in you, too, as a dear friend."

"Kelly, can...can I like tell you a secret you might need to know?"

"Please."

Davey sighed. I'm older than Tom cause like I changed majors. See. I have an eye for stock and bonds and shit, so I'm a year from finishing my degree in that even though I'm like ancient," he said as he chuckled. Before that, I did what my dad wanted and was pre-med. I ain't shit good at first aid, like I can do the basics only, but if you need me...."

Kelly grinned and replied, "That's the best news I've had since all of this went bad. I suspected something when I saw Tyrese's bandages. I knew something was going on, you stinker. Check Vera's leg because she hates me, and be sure there's no infection. See if she is allergic to penicillin, and if she doesn't know, ask if she is allergic to bees. If she isn't allergic to bees, then she probably isn't allergic to penicillin, but I have benedryl, just in case. Give her a shot for me?"

Davey nodded and said, "No problem. That's simple. I won't let you down. I'll get the shot in her, get her high on a doobie, and get her to sleep. I can do that."

In reality, he actually did exactly that, and Vera fell asleep without pain and finally rested comfortably. She didn't argue about smoking drugs once she understood the pain would go away; coughing, she smoked and took the shot and lay down with a huge smile on her face.

Soup was set aside for Vera and the captain because they would awaken later, but the rest dug in, and there was a small bit of crispy fried fish for each. Joe and Fish began to devise ways to set crab traps and traps for shellfish. After eating, they swam out, and soon, the traps and lines were set and would hopefully provide food.

Joe nodded happily and said, "The sea will provide us with nutritious food that tastes good and can be used in many different recipes. I can make coconut shrimp if we get both ingredients. Seaweed can help make sushi, very healthy stuff."

After several attempts in designing, Scott and Tom made a sled that they mounted on waterskies, huge, and yet, not heavy. Tom also asked Tyrese for help in constructing the thing so that it could carry a lot of supplies and weight but added little weight of its own. *It could bog down, but mostly it would glide over the dry sand and zip fast over the wet sand. It wouldn't be perfect, but they would use it to scout for supplies that washed up and down the beach,* he thought.

Scott, Helen, Tyrese, Alex, Joy, and Tom were on that team, leaving the rest to catch food, scavenge for supplies, tend to the injured, and defend the camp. How the team came to be was odd. Tyrese and Tom asked Scott and Alex because they were the best dinosaur experts they had, Helen volunteered, and Joy offered to go. All of them got along before the wreck and figured they could as a salvage team, too.

Vaughn gave his brother Tom a nod and smirked; Stu was constructing a bow and arrows.

"Joe came from that way, so let's look." Tom pointed. In a short time, they had picked up items in the sea trash that washed up. There were several tee shirts, some socks, five flat air mattresses in various conditions, a full bottle of sunscreen, many empty and full water bottles, towels and sheets, and one broken, useless cell phone. Their big find was a few sealed packets of mixed nuts, bruised lemons and limes, some plastic bottles of liquor, and two of the bar stools. The legs of those would make excellent weapons. The padded seats would be good chairs for sitting in the sand.

They found three duffle bags, a few small beach bags, and four backpacks. It was a gold strike. Because they had found so much and some of the blankets were wet and heavy and took up so much room, they had to stop and take all of what they had back to the camp.

As soon as they dumped that haul, they went back out. They found a few other items that had washed up, but nothing was like they had found in the first haul.

They stopped when they found a mutilated body. It was hard to say who it was, but they thought it might be one of the missing crew members. He had been okay enough to start a tiny fire, but before night had come and the others had seen it, something had attacked the man.

"His head is just gone. It wasn't chewed away; it was snapped off, see?" said Alex as he showed them.

"Yuk. What does that mean?" Joy asked.

"Look here at the stomach. Whatever it was had a big mouth, and it wanted the soft organs as well as the brains."

"Those troodons last night had big mouths," Helen said.

"It looked like that, I know, but this thing would be three times that big. Look at the footprint here."

"That's a footprint?" asked Joy as her pretty eyes went big.

"I'm afraid so, Joy," Alex said, "I would guess this thing is twenty feet tall. If this is a small island, then that may be as large as they get, but it's a big one." From the sand, he picked up long, brown feathers with violet-blue tips that were wet with blood and seawater.

"What is it?"

Alex shrugged and answered, "I have no idea. Something big, but not as big as a T-Rex or an allosaurus. It is a smaller meat eater and kind of picky to leave the rest here." Alex searched the area, and he called out, "He's a lone hunter. We should avoid him since he attacks in the day light so that makes him very brave."

Alex, always one to know useless trivia, found purslane growing on the rocks and gathered it, eating some as he worked since there was more than they could take back. He told them it was rich in nutrients and could be chopped and added to soup, wrapped around fish to steam, used to stuff fish or make a salad, cooked with vegetables, or eaten raw.

"This is pretty good," Joy said as she ate some, "but it needs vinegar, oil, salt, and pepper, and maybe some garlic. Yum. With steak or liver...delish."

"Well, you let Joe know. If we find wine, we can get vinegar, right?"

Alex led the way to the trees. They listened and looked, but there was no movement. He nodded and walked farther into the shadows. Coconuts littered the ground. "These won't have as much water, but the meat will be fine. And those are sea grapes. They're really delicious, I've heard." He tried one, spitting out the big seed. It was good. He pointed out wild onions and picked them.

Scott, Helen, Tyrese, Joy, and Tom ate the sea grapes and agreed that they were delicious. They finished their snack and gathered the sea grapes and coconuts.

"I don't know much about survival in the wild, but I saw a show; give me a few minutes." Scott grinned as he attacked a tree, cutting off the upper branches and then cutting below so that he had a huge section of tree. Everyone had to help him pull it out to the beach so that he could see better to work. They frowned and ate sea grapes as they watched, thinking he was crazy to be working so hard at the big log section of tree.

Scott pointed and said, "We can take it back although it will take work, but I'm getting some to show you. On T.V. the work was easier." He poured sweat. Removing several layers of bark, he got to the middle of the tree and cut out a fat section that he held up. He was tired after all of that but determined to finish.

He sliced it apart and handed pieces to everyone.

"Okay, here goes," said Joy as she took a bite. She smiled around her piece and kept eating. "This will go with my purslane salad perfectly."

"Oh, it's like the heart of palm, like an artichoke," Helen said. The palm was tender and slightly sweet. It tasted wonderful. "We need vinegar and salt water, and then we can pickle it with some seasonings."

"By the way, that big tree I cut will be a lot of food, but I dulled Joe's knife and will have to sharpen it again for him. I know we have fish and what we have scavenged, but this alone will feed us. We won't starve," Scott said.

Alex nodded. "You out did me."

"No, I added variety is all."

"We need water," Helen reminded them.

"Look for a trail. There should be one that animals use." Tyrese looked for one, being careful not to run into a dinosaur.

In a few minutes, Helen waved the others to her, and she showed them a packed, worn trail. Leaving the sled, they followed it, listening for sounds and holding weapons close.

"Shhhh." Tyrese held his hand up. They faintly heard water flowing over rocks. They carefully followed the sounds, trying to be quiet.

"That's a hadrosaur."

"Does it eat plants or people?" Joy asked.

Alex smiled and answered, "Plants. I think it could be a maiasaura. They are not mean, but if we scare them, they could run us over. Be quiet."

The creatures smelled humans, something they were not used to. They sniffed and snorted. There were five of them, all about twenty feet long from duck-bill to tail-tip. Colored soft green, they could easily hide in the trees and foliage. They had mouths that were like that of a duck, rounded heads, and soft looking bodies; they acted like cattle.

"If we can't catch fish or just want another food, we can take down a small one," Tom said.

"I was just thinking that," Helen agreed.

They moved slowly, filling bottles and containers with the water. For now, it would have to be boiled to make sure it was safe to drink, but there might be a time when they would have to drink it like the animals did. The water came from farther in the trees and from some unknown source, but it rippled across rocks and formed a small, fast moving creek. It looked clean.

"We have to come back and follow this one way or the other. Maybe there is a pool so we can bathe," Tom said.

The hadrosaurs jerked, their heads rose, and they cocked their heads. One snorted, and their bodies went tense.

"Is it us?" Joy asked.

Alex motioned for everyone to retreat and hide behind some fallen trees. He had a bad feeling as he watched the hadrosaurs react to something they heard or smelled. The birds had gone silent.

Coming from the greenery and pushing past vines and bushes, a bigger creature appeared. He stood twenty feet tall and was solid muscle. Although his front legs were small, he made up for it with his huge back legs and the sharp claws on his big toes. He was brown, and along his spine were brown feathers, tipped with a pretty blue.

"What is he? A T-Rex?" Joy whispered as she asked.

"No. He isn't. He isn't an allosaurus, either." Alex ran every book, every television show, and all Internet images through his head. Nothing matched. This beast's legs and lower body were far heavier and bigger than in any pictures of dinosaurs Amex had ever seen. He wasn't a runner. This animal didn't chase prey because he was far too heavy, but his mode of killing was lethal.

He crept up and used his size to knock his prey to the ground so that he could use a big back claw to pin them. They might fight back, but he also had a thick, short neck and could use it to deflect blows and rip out a throat. He was the bully of this environment, always stalking and unafraid of any other beast.

He sniffed.

The hadrosaurs were frozen. If they moved, he would leap. They backed away, but Big Brown advanced, stepping through the creek and muddying the waters with his big feet.

The hadrosaurs broke and tried to run, and four got away, fleeing as fast as possible, but the Big Brown lunged, slinging himself at the lone hadrosaur and and knocking it down. The slowest and the dumbest most often die, thereby not sharing those faulty genetics nor strengthening the species.

The victim screamed, making all the birds take flight. The thud was loud in the woods, and it was effective as the brown predator stomped and battered with his foot and with his neck and chest. In an easy motion, Big Brown leaned in and ripped a huge chunk from the hadrosaur's throat and gulped down the flesh.

The creek turned bright red as blood jetted and poured from the lethal wound. The hadrosaur kicked and fought weakly, but the size of the animals made it sound as if a full war were in progress. There were thuds and bangs, snaps and snorts, but it ended in a few minutes that felt like forever to those who watched.

Big Brown, as everyone thought of him, leaned in and immediately began to eviscerate the hadrosaur, taking enormous bites of the belly. Because he killed so easily, he could be a picky eater, only wanting the best parts of the body. He was a loud eater, snapping bones and smacking up fat and strings of intestines, so the group of humans were able to slowly and almost silently back away.

They didn't speak until they were a long way from the butchery.

"Oh my, God, Big Brown, he's...." Joy stopped and vomited the sea grapes and purslane onto the trail.

"Now we know. What is he, Alex?" Tom asked. He wanted to know what kind of *dinosaur* this was. He accepted the word, now, because those could be nothing else, weren't hidden by the night shadows, and looked like pictures in books. At least the hadrosaurs did.

"I've thought and thought, but I don't think anyone has ever found a fossil of him. He's different. Have you noticed that he is bottom heavy and short?"

Helen snorted. "Short? He's huge."

"He's short compared to many we could find. Trust me, he's small. All are built differently. I think it's some adaptation." Alex waited as Joy finished being sick. "I have no name for him but *Big Brown*. He's bold. We have to be on guard because he is the type that would walk right into camp for a kill."

Joy wiped her mouth and looked at the others with tears on her face and said, "I'm scared."

"I am, too," Tyrese said, "but they are just animals. We can outsmart them. We may have to go after him before he comes to us."

Scott nodded. He thought the same thing.

"Hey, is this your knife? Why…." Joy reached into the moss beside the trail and picked up a knife that was a foot long, handle to tip. She was about to ask why it was rusted and whom it belonged to, but suddenly she knew it wasn't theirs. She wasn't sure what this meant. But it chilled her.

Scott looked at the knife he took from her, turning it over in his hands. "Now why would this be here? Why? A random knife on a trail."

"Because someone has been here before us," Tom said. He rubbed at his wounded arm, irritated by the itchy feeling. His mind whirled. "We aren't the first, and why would we be?"

Alex nodded and replied, "Right. That's true."

Joy frowned and slid closer to Alex; she thought he was smart and made her feel safe. "And?"

He patted her shoulder and blushed. He was kind of amazed that she had noticed him. "People were or are here and are also stranded. Someone lost this knife, and I think it's been out here a few months. That means they may or may not be alive." He tried to cover the variables.

"Maybe they were rescued."

"We'd have heard about it, Joy."

Joy frowned at Tom and looked at Alex and asked, "Do you agree?"

"Yeah. I don't think anyone was rescued. I think since the water is ruined from that spot and down, we'll have to go deeper into the trees. We might find out about the other people."

"*If* we want to find them," Helen said.

"Why wouldn't we?"

Helen didn't know, but it was a thought that just popped into her head. "Maybe they aren't nice people, or maybe the island has driven them crazy. We should just be careful and try to see them before they see us, I mean if they are alive and if we can find them."

"I agree," Tyrese said, "all of you may not be seeing it, but we have our own people who are a little...." He twirled his finger at his temple.

"My sister," Tom said, "nuts. And my dad, he isn't right, is he? I thought it was shock or something, but Kelly said his head injuries are bad. His head was knocked around a lot, and he isn't right. He just sits and stares and pats Vera. Half the time, he doesn't notice if I call his name."

"I'm sorry, Tom," Helen said, "but Stu is himself, and he scares me at times. He is so...."

"*Angry*," Tom supplied the word, " or jealous? Mean? I know. He worries me as well. My entire family, except Vaughn, is useless."

Helen wiped away a tear as they walked down the trail. Scott reached over and with one arm and hugged her, and she leaned into him. She wanted to stop and have him hold her while she cried for everyone, everything, and herself, but there wasn't time. He seemed to know as he pulled her close but didn't quite kiss her cheek, only brushed his face against her skin, letting her know he understood.

Watching behind them for Big Brown, they finished loading the sled with water and everything else they found: more sea grapes and coconuts and several dozen mangoes. The sled was heavy as they strained, pulling the sled along on the sand, but the work was worth it to have the supplies.

After a long time, they saw camp and found new energy to pull the load along with them. Tyrese waved at the ones back at camp, and they waved back, excited to see what was on the sled this time.

Scott thought about the rusty knife. "Wait until they hear we're not alone."

Chapter 5: Day 2 Evening

The new and unusual food delighted most of the survivors as they tasted everything and chatted about it, but this wasn't a taste-test situation. The camp, although filled with useful supplies, was pitiful with the wreckage as a home and junk as treasures.

Alex told the story of the scavenging trip, making sure everyone understood that Big Brown was dangerous and that they had to be vigilant. Sue thought about everything she knew and agreed that it sounded as if Big Brown were a new kind of dinosaur, undiscovered in fossils. "They will name it after you, Alex."

"Cool, but I don't think he is mine, really."

While the rest were gone, Amanda and Fish organized the camp and set up a system for guard duty. Amanda was bandaged, and she mourned the loss of her fingers, but she also willed the wound to heal and threw herself into her job of keeping everyone calm and safe.

Kelly checked wounds as soon as they arrived and found everyone was fine, except Tom whose slashed arm was worrisome. His flesh was tender, itched, and was bright red. She gave him one of the last of the penicillin shots, and as he grimaced, she scrubbed the injury again since she thought it was getting infected. She slept that night in his arms, worrying and restless. He told her he was there for her and to relax.

Stanley sat with the injured, scared to be outside the wreckage. He wondered about his choice to volunteer since Vera complained and whined. After his guard duty, Davey came over and sat with her, relieving Stanley. He lit a marijuana cigarette and shared with her.

"That's illegal."

"So? Like who cares, Dude? She's in pain."

"They are still drugs."

Davey narrowed his eyes and said, "You wanted to sit with the injured so you didn't have guard duty. Being a coward is worse than a little toke. Don't judge me." He didn't realize his speech had altered and that he wasn't in the persona of *stoner*. His emotional protection was down as he grew angry.

"I can't fight one of those things. Jeez. I'm a computer geek."

"So?"

"So I'm scared. Okay? There. I'm a big coward and scared. I can't help what I am."

Davey saw tears running down Stanley's face, and he softened. "We're all scared, Dude."

"Does that drug help her?"

Vera smiled and said, "Yeah. Have you seen her leg? No? It's not pretty, and it hurts like hell, so if this helps her, why not?"

"Davey, light another, please?" Vera begged.

He sighed but did as asked. "You want?" He offered it to Stanley.

"No, thanks, the captain says he wants him back him on his feet in the morning. That's good. About Durango, he doesn't say anything."

"His head is binged up," said Vera, giggling, "he's messed up."

"Maybe he'll get better," Davey said.

Vera shook her head and replied, "No bing, bing. He's lost it. That's a body, but Daddy died in the wreck." Tears ran down her cheeks as she giggled, and with huge eyes, she looked at Davey.

He understood what she meant.

Davey understood a lot. He got what they were saying. They might be problematic, but they were who they were and not cut out for this extreme situation.

In the corner, Pamela rested but awoke often reaching for her face. She was bruised black and green, had a dozen stitched gashes, and looked like a patchwork quilt. Finding a mirror, she looked at her injuries and started screaming. Amanda and Kelly had hell trying to get her to stop screaming and touching her stitches. Each time she awoke, she moaned that she was an ugly monster.

That lodged in her head, and she thought about the troodons who killed Wanda. She began to repeat a mantra: *"Monster Island, Monster Island, Monster Island."*

Stanley begged her to stop before Stu heard her again and started raving.

In the shadows away from the fire, Joy and Alex pretended to be on guard duty but made frantic love in the sand. Joy demanded and took, and when they were finished the second time, Alex felt used. Joy had taken something, but he wasn't sure what it was. Stu winked at him and smirked. Tom rolled his eyes. Tyrese whispered that it was about time Alex joined the club of men who had been with her. Fish held up his thumb.

Alex stalked away to the other side of the fire and told Joy he wanted to be alone so he could guard the camp like he was supposed to.

Helen slept next to Scott, and in her sleep, she rolled close. He smiled.

Fish announced he wanted to help explore. "It is no accident we are here. Others have had the same fate. We must find out who owns this island: man or beast."

Durango Jones, unable to hold thoughts and unsure how to get thoughts to words, nodded solemnly. For a fraction of a second, his head stopped pounding, and his mind cleared. *We are meat*, he thought. What he thought was unimportant.

Day three was coming.

Chapter 5: Day 3

Joe's cooking helped fill everyone's bellies with a Louisiana-inspired fish stew, palms and fried squid, and coconut with crab. The group ate well, but the scavenging crew had no time to stay and visit: they had to gear up and set out again. They had two backpacks and make-shift knapsacks. It was the same team as before except Fish went along. Fish took over somewhat on the scavenging mission. The objective was to fill water bottles with fresh water as it was found and to look for signs of other people.

That left Amanda as crew-member-in-charge-of-the-camp.

The group liked having Fish go with them because he was tall, strong, and smart. However, Joy was the weak link; she kind of worked hard and was one of the few who was unhurt, willing to go, and not needed at camp because she didn't do well with fishing.

"Thanks, Joe, I'm stuffed."

"And it is all fresh; I am glad to cook for you," Joe told Scott. "These foods you brought me made the flavors. That coconut...very delicious."

The group walked away from camp and showed Fish all they had seen before. They wanted to walk down the beach and search along the shore, but finding water seemed more important. If they had to travel far, the trips could be tiring and dangerous.

Tyrese pointed out to Fish where they had found the rusty knife and explained it again. Fish looked at the knife, but there was nothing else there to find or figure out. Fish carefully ran probing fingers through the moss and under the leaves, but there was nothing.

"I puked there," Joy said, conversationally.

They walked to the creek and found the rotting hadrosaur, its body ruining all the water that rushed around it and past it, gurgling and lapping at the banks. They boiled the water they gathered, but the idea of drinking water that was filled with decay and feces was unnerving, and they didn't want that on their hands or in the bottles.

"I thought scavengers would eat it," Helen said.

Alex nodded and said, "They will. He was a big animal, and Big Brown pissed all over it to keep them away. In a few days or when it rains, they will finish him to the bone."

"But the bones will remain, so we have to see them and remember. Yuk," Joy said.

Nothing was at the creek drinking. So the group moved cautiously along the animal trail, following the creek. Sometimes the water almost vanished among large rocks, but then they saw it again. A trail branched off, and it caught their attention because several of the trees had been cut down, and they knew this because instead of tooth prints, they saw the cuts left by a knife or machete.

"Again, people have been here," Alex told them.

"We can get water here. It's clean. Let's find out what's down this trail."

"As long as it isn't Big Brown, right Alex?"

Alex nodded at Joy, blushing. He wasn't sure how he felt about her in the daylight. He was confused and deep in his own thoughts.

"How's the arm?" Helen asked Tom. She saw him rubbing at it. He shrugged and turned away. "Hey," she said as she clutched his shoulder and leaned closer.

"I didn't let Kelly see and avoided her 'cause she'll worry." I was too busy, so I hurried along. I think she's out of antibiotics anyway.

He held out his arm, and Helen's eyes went wide. The gauze was matted in spots with a yellow-green crust. Tom took some gauze out of his pocket; it wasn't sterile anymore, but that hardly mattered, and he wrapped a few layers around his arm to hide the infection. Tom's eyes were glassy with fever and worry. He wasn't so much afraid for himself but was terrified for Kelly. Who would care for her if something happened to him? That nagged at him continuously.

"Does your arm hurt much? Are you sore in your arm pit?"

"Yeah, both, but then I kind of rub my arm and mash it, and it…well…the infection comes out some. Hurts when I do, but I do it. I know that it isn't good, but what can I do? She cleaned it. She gave me a shot. It's one of those things I can't do anything about. At least it's draining. That's got to be better than not draining, right?"

Helen nodded. She felt in her pocket, handed him a package of aspirin, and watched as he swallowed them.

While walking on the trail that wound through the trees, they found some sea grapes and mangoes to take back. When they came back down the path, they would gather them. Boulders marked the next trail split. On a whim, they went left because it looked the most used.

Three compsognathus were eating sea grapes while sitting on the trail, and they ran away, chattering and fussing at the humans. They were smaller than the ones before, and Alex said they looked like juveniles, maybe. Tyrese threw a rock, missing them as they ran.

The trees thickened, and the group saw a very small swampy area, no bigger than a small horse's footprint. It was a slimy, gooey mess that smelled rank, and black sludge and fungus lined the banks. Probably once it had been a clear pond of sorts but had since gone bad with something: animal droppings, rotting vegetation, and algae. That was what it smelled and looked like. It was a filthy pool, but the miasma of stink covered other scents as well. Some animals would be almost hidden in the stink.

To the other side of the pool was a more worn area, with trampled moss and dirt in a small clearing. Undergrowth and vines were gone, and the trees were pushed away or uprooted and tossed into the swamp. Several creatures or something large must live in there; the smell of danger was there. The tactic worked well because nothing would wish to be here for very long.

"Be careful about quicksand," Fish warned. He watched the ground, wondering at all the dangers that lurked. Small, shiny-backed beetles raced around the grubby ground, darting among old brown broken twigs and leaves and working among the bits of bark. They weren't common-looking bugs, but they were not monstrous either, yet the little bugs still made the people feel crawly and threatened. The beetles might be perfectly safe, but they brought a feeling of revulsion to Fish as he saw them.

"Those are icky bugs," Joy said. That seemed to summarize them excellently. The bugs were but a small part, yet this whole place was bad. Everyone felt that.

Alex tilted his head and motioned everyone to stop.

He thought there was a circular area that was delineated by sticks and dead grass and immediately decided this was a nest. Whether it was active or old was another question. Scott and he decided to slide between rocks and trees and get a better look. Almost at once, Scott pointed to a big, stinky pile of feces, and they began to notice more piles around the circular area. They were fresh, a few hours old, maybe, and covered by loud blowflies.

Scott made a face and said, "Climb up so we can see without going closer." They found foot and handholds and climbed the rocks on the opposite side of the circle across from the swamp.

From their vantage point far off the ground, they could see the nest, a huge one. Egg shells littered the nest, and Alex mentally began to put the large shells together so he could guess at a size of them. They had to be at least two feet long and almost half that wide.

Scott sucked in his next breath, and Alex wondered what was wrong.

He followed Scott's gaze to one side. "Oh my, God. Those are human bones. Look at the two skulls." Alex gagged. A lot of bones were there probably those of smaller dinosaurs, but two skulls were tossed to the side as if Alex and Scott were meant to find them.

"A month? Two? Can you tell? They aren't fresh as in a week or two, but they aren't yellowed and mossy, either, like the other bones."

"A-month-old, I think. I'd have to hold them and see, but no way in hell am I going into that." He did the math. "A month ago...maybe two...the babies hatched, and the parents fed them." Alex gagged again. For some reason he thought of Joy and making love, and he became nauseated. How could he forget where he was and indulge in that last night when they were in danger of being the next meal for dinosaurs. One minute they were people and the next meat for monsters.

He knew he had to suppress his physical desire and stop any emotions he was beginning to feel for her, and he did have feelings, or he wouldn't have had sex with her. Feelings had no place on this island. There was only survival.

He went on, "By now, the parents will be teaching them to hunt. That's where they are: hunting."

"Where?"

"How the fuck would I know, Scott? What a stupid question," Alex said as he rubbed his head, still sick.

"Okay. Fair enough. Can you guess...just guess what these are?"

Alex stared at the egg shells. They were huge. He ruled out the velociraptor because of the large size. "Maybe, Utahraptor. Or it's one that is similar. Who knows if it's a known species. Let's say it is. They are big. Sorry. My head aches right now, and I feel sick. I shouldn't have snapped at you and cursed. I feel so disgusted."

"It's fine."

The Utahraptors were enormous. When fully grown, they measured twenty-five feet from snout to tail tip. People often knew what a velociraptor was and were terrified of them, but velociraptors only weighed about two hundred pounds. The Utahraptor weighed a half ton; they were the largest raptors of all.

And Alex knew something else about them, theory or not. He leaned down and asked, "T-Dog, can you and Fish get everyone up here on the rocks? You need to climb, and I mean right this second. Fast. Hurry." His voice became louder. Had they gone back down the trail, they would have run into a hunting pack. There was nowhere to go but upwards unless they wished to dig under the leaves with the bugs; it was a blind, dead-end alley.

What a brilliant hunting strategy. Alex admired the skill even as he feared it and hated it. They were in so much danger, and the urgency was enough to almost suffocate Alex. No wonder he had felt so nauseated and then angry and irritable; at some level, he was aware as any prey would be.

Helen reached for a sturdy rock and started climbing immediately, knowing this was a serious situation.

Joy said she couldn't climb and asked why they had to. She wasted a few seconds complaining and questioning why she had to climb rocks when there was nothing up there she wanted to see.

Alex wanted to reach down and slap her for taking so long to get moving. There was no time to explain everything he saw and felt in his sick, terrified bowels and stomach.

Tyrese wasn't playing games, so he grabbed Joy, raised her above his head, and told her to grab a rock because he was letting go. She complained but clutched the rocks. He almost slammed her into the rocks as he got her going.

"I can't; damn, T-Dog, I can't climb with this arm," Tom said, "so leave me. Go on." Tom meant it. He didn't want to slow them down, and he wasn't sure if he could climb with his arm so messed up.

"I have broken fingers, but the man said climb, and that is what *we* will do."

"Move. Get going. I will help, you, Tom," said Fish as he began to climb beside Tom, finding rocks that they both could use to climb. "That is how you do it. Keep moving. Up the rocks, we go."

"Climb!" Scott yelled this time; he looked down with big eyes and kept looking at those climbing and then off behind them.

Heavy thuds made it clear that something big ran towards the humans. The Utahraptors were coming, and they squealed and shrieked their pleasure, hoping to terrify their prey into freezing in place. They didn't need that, but it never hurt to have an easy kill. This close to the nest and with babies in the pack hunting, a fast kill was far more favorable to them than a long, violent battle would be.

Still urging the rest to hurry, Scott climbed down and helped Helen climb up the rest of the way, yanking her up as he went. He didn't question where his strength was coming from. He was so scared that his heart hammered as if it would explode from his chest. He didn't see the faces of those creatures attacking, but their happy roars were terrifying. They were excited about ripping into fresh meat.

Alex didn't think but just climbed over to help Joy and Tom. "T-Dog, get Joy up."

"You bet." He yanked her over the rocks like a rag doll, scraping her flesh over the sharp, rough rocks. Blood spots smeared in patches, her skin scraped off, and she howled, but Tyrese never stopped. He kept pulling her upwards, far past where Scott and Alex had watched the nest.

The screams of the excited animals and the screams of pain coming from Joy combined and filled the area.

"You're hurting me."

"Climb." Alex didn't let go of Joy.

Fish pushed Tom upwards as Tom tried to find handholds, but one of Tom's arms was weak and caused him pain. He wasn't able to hold on and then use the arm before he lost the hold, groaning with pain. Green infection leaked through his bandage. He was frustrated with the weakness in his arm. The cacophony didn't make him rush; it made him afraid to move any faster for fear he would lose his grip and fall among the raptors.

Tom was brave, always, but the screeches and roars made his already weak body feel wispy and unsubstantial. He didn't know how to make his limbs work anymore.

The Utahraptors came as a full pack: the huge adults, the juveniles born a year earlier who had survived the hard conditions, and the little ones, the babies who were five feet tall. Each was streamlined, muscular, but built tightly. From foot to head, they were eight feet tall, and they were greyish green, grey, and beige. Each forearm ended with long, knife-like claws and long feathers that were birdlike but far too sparse, making them have *hand-wings*. Their mouths were birdlike as well, but they had impressive teeth since they were so large.

But their secret weapon, the trait they were known for, was on their back feet, a sickle-shaped, razor-sharp, twelve-inch-long claw. They could use that claw without moving the rest of their toes. Paleontologists knew it was a lethal weapon, but it was more frightening to see it on the animal.

Click, click, click went the claws on the rocks.

Tyrese popped one in the eye when the creature came too close, trying to climb. The eyeball popped out in a mess of goo, and the animal fell back to the ground. He roared back as he fell. Tyrese felt elated and sick.

"Go, Fish."

"We will be lucky, Tom. Keep climbing, and we will be there."

Alex yanked at Tom, pulled him along, and they made progress.

"A little more. They can't climb worth shit. Come on, Tom."

Tom shook his head. Below, Fish had slapped Tom's foot into a deep foot hole that would keep him safe until he found the next one. Tom was already mapping out the rest of the way with Alex, but Fish held his foot.

"Fish?"

"I have an unfortunate, unlucky situation, Tom Jones. When I let you go, I will have but one hand grasping the rocks," Fish groaned and made another terrible noise.

Alex shifted and saw what was wrong.

A Utahraptor had one of Fish's lower legs gripped tightly in his mouth but couldn't budge his prey since Fish fought to stay away. Another of the monsters had snagged Fish's other foot, and it was pulling; it had locked razor-like nails into Fish's ankle.

"Gonna lose two feet, and we have no fire to stop the bleeding. This is not a good place, and I am unlucky today."

"Fish, don't let go," Tom called down. He believed there had to be a way out of this, but he still cried softly as he understood the problem. Fish was like family to him.

"Meh, he will climb up my body and get you. I think that is unacceptable. Letting go, and Alex, you yank his ass as far as you can. Do not let this be for nothing, yes?" The pain was far away for him as his body went into shock; he was indeed lucky in this way. His injuries already were so bad that the nerves were numbed. Fish knew he had no chance and was at peace. It wasn't for nothing that he would die.

Alex gulped. He was a science geek. He was majoring in science and history and was no hero. Without hesitation, he called, "On three, be at peace, friend."

"No," Tom screamed, "not for me. I am sick anyway. No."

"Two." Alex ignored him and was on the second number before Tom could think of a way out of this. Alex understood.

Fish and Alex yelled at the same time, "Three."

Fish removed his hand, Tom went flying upwards as Alex yanked him. "Fish?"

"I can not hold on."

The two creatures yanked again, and Fish fell right between them. One immediately sliced his gut open, and Fish screamed long and loud as his guts boiled from his belly. Another creature chomped into the intestines and ran, making the intestines stretch along like a rope. From the side, baby Utahraptors ran out and grabbed the goodies they wanted most.

One big creature pulled and yanked at Fish's leg until he ripped it from the hip socket. Another tore away a hand, and the one after him took the entire arm. A small juvenile was clever and sneaky, and he waited for a slight body roll and then bit into Fish's tender, lower back on the side, going for the kidney, a favorite treat. Fish still screamed.

He drew a breath and yelled, "We're meat."

It was the first contraction he had used since he was a small child with a mother that taught him at home and said contractions made a person sound ignorant and uneducated. Somehow, it didn't matter. It was as close to cursing as Fish had ever come.

Those on the rocks moved away, refusing to watch anymore of the attack. Each wanted to kill all the monsters; they hated them. Fish stopped screaming when the rest of the humans got to the top of the rocks. They sank down in a circle and sat, staring at nothing.

Joy cried hysterically all over Tyrese; he was too devastated and tired to push her away, and besides he wasn't that cruel. Helen sat so that Scott was able to wrap both arms around her and they could cry and whisper their fears and sadness; Helen cried hard.

Tom sat and punched his leg, then picked at his bandage, cursed, and punched more. He cried over Fish.

Alex sat alone, his face toward where they had been. He saw nothing and took time to pray to a God he had given up years before. He prayed hard, hoping to be heard. "Scott, again, let me say I am so sorry I snapped and cursed at you. Fish never said anything like what I yelled. I am sorry."

"Stop. It's okay." Scott nodded solemnly.

"He was the best. He was strong. Why Fish?"

"Tom, he knew what he was doing. All of us are in a bad place, and it could have been any one of us. He was brave, and we should understand that that was how he wanted to stay. He couldn't have lived with anything less," Scott said.

"We could have, though," Tom was petulant. He felt guilty and angry. He was scared and sad. He was also growing more feverish and berated himself for this additional weakness.

They stayed there for an hour, and then Scott suggested everyone take food and water from his own pack and eat and drink.

The water wasn't boiled. *Come on cholera or typhoid fever. E Coli? Sure,* Scott thought.

Tyrese bandaged Joy's scrapes as best he could, but some were impossible to dress because they were so very painful yet were only skinned places. Helen unwrapped Tom's arm and caught her breath. The gash wasn't very long and was closed in most places, but all around, it was deep red and purple. Helen pressed, and thick, slimy infection popped out at once. She pressed all over, despite his protests, and wiped and scrubbed away a huge amount of infection.

Without a word, Alex handed over his flask of rum and shrugged.

Forcing the wound open again, Helen used it to clean the wound and rub away skin that looked as if it were dying. Tom was red faced with fever, but he went pale.

"Give me your coconut and the purslane you have; I don't need a lot." After cutting them up, Helen packed both into the gash. She added some rum and wrapped all of it in a bandage.

Tom groaned and moaned.

"So?"

"Well, T, I'm not a doctor, and I don't know anything, but they both are nutritious to eat and have good things in them, so why not? I'm out of ideas, and the man who could do what might have to be done just died." Helen wanted to sit and cry again. She doubted either of what she packed into the wound would help, but she was out of ideas. She felt that they needed Fish so much, but he was gone.

"You're not taking my arm."

"I think there are red streaks beginning."

Tom spat and said, "I don't care. You aren't taking it. Let me die if it gets to that. I won't stand it. No one will do that to me."

"Oh, Tom!" Joy slid over and lay against him, holding him close.

Tyrese winked at Alex. "We need to get out of here. These rocks are useful. We can go that way to see if we can get to the other trail and then back track to where the trail splits, then get water, and get out of here."

"Tom needs rest," Helen said, "so can we scout it out, and then half way there, some can come back and get him? Then, we can go the rest of the way to something? Let's be sure we have a place to go."

"He can't stay alone, but Helen, you're coming with me, period," Scott said. She didn't argue. They both picked up the few weapons they had tossed up onto the rocks as they climbed. Helen handed hers to Tyrese. Alex was going because he understood the creatures the most.

"Joy, can you stay with him and *be* calm and keep *him* calm?" Scott asked. "We need you to do this one thing."

"I can! I'll help Tom! Poor thing, so sick."

"Ok, give us about half an hour, no more than an hour...'k?" Tyrese asked.

"Got it, T," Joy said as she nodded.

The others left, looking back a few times. The raptors had finished and had taken the scraps back to the nest, but they couldn't see any of that. They looked back but were glad they couldn't see Fish's remains. It wasn't something easy explained, but they couldn't stop looking; maybe they were scared the raptors might be coming after them, sneaking along the rocks.

The ground was easy to walk over, and a sort of trail was there that Alex thought compys used to stay away from the big predators. Little dinosaurs could run a long way without being in reach of the deadly claws of the big creatures.

"A trail down! The biggies can't walk that with twists and turns, but compys and people can." Helen felt hopeful.

"Hey, look over here. Is that a cave?"

"I think so. It makes sense there would be a place to hide up here where it's safer from big things," Helen said to Scott.

They followed Scott. A woven gate of some type had fallen over and was dusty. It made them feel there was no one there. But the weaving work made it clear that someone *had been*.

"Hello!" they called out, but it was quiet.

Tyrese held a hand out to warn them to wait as he got a fire going to light the room. Someone had left kindling and large pieces of wood in a fire pit near the entrance. He wanted light to see by; they didn't need any shocks.

There were threadbare, blue blankets, but only a few. Some cushions that matched the blankets and leaked stuffing as well as some clothing were stacked neatly, along with a few suitcases, a few cups, plates, and random items, and then there was some junk littering the camp. Spears were set against one wall, but it looked as if half of the weapons had been removed because of the way they leaned in a line with gaps where none were. Animal bones, clean and bleached, were in a pile along the cave's side. If there had been food, small animals had taken it.

"There's been no one here for a month or two. Maybe they are the ones…you know…back there." Scott had to stop and tell the rest what they saw in the nest and what the dinosaur was called.

"In the nest?" Helen asked as she shivered, "that's sickening. I know they are animals, but it makes me scared to think of them here, preying on people."

"See the logo? I think this was a small plane," said Alex as he kicked a cushion, making dust fly.

"Didn't Southern Flights lose a plane a few months ago? Remember? They looked all over the Bermuda Triangle and around Florida and then said it was high jacked and had crashed."

"I remember that, Scott," Helen said as she dug around, feeling there was more, and then she held up a little book. "Ah, ha! We have a diary. We can find out who they were and what happened."

"You are sharp. Now, let's take the knives and the spears; they don't need them," Tyrese said, "anything else?"

"The blankets are rather ratty. The cups? Plates?" Helen slid everything into her rucksack. She shook her head at the pile of dead cell phones. "I feel as if there were quite a few people here at one time. You saw the remains of two. I wonder what happened?"

"I think we can guess," Scott said.

"You have a diary, so we'll find out."

Helen nodded to Alex and said, "I thought there might be one. I should be keeping one. I'll start one soon."

Alex smiled sadly and responded, "We know the way down. Let's go get Tom and Joy, get water, and take Tom to Kelly to see if she can save his arm, and then eat some eel tonight. Joe promised.

Helen made a face, and they went back to get the other two of their group.

"And we have to tell the rest about Fish," Tyrese added as they walked, "I dread that. I feel as if we failed."

As soon as they rounded a boulder, they had a surprise.

Joy was standing beside Tom and was just slipping on her panties. Her shorts were on the ground. Tom's shirt was removed, and his shorts were down by his feet. They were talking quietly.

Helen stood still for a second and stared. She was shocked. Then she was off, moving fast, and she walked past the men and got to the small camp first. She stood straight and pointed a finger at Joy and asked, "What are you doing *NOW*?"

"I…we…don't you *yell* at me. He's hurting and sick, and I made him feel *better*. I think his fever broke."

"If so, it was because of something else. How could you? You know he is going to propose to Kelly." Helen helped pull Tom's pants up, fastened them, and put his shirt back on him. Dully, he watched her, but he did help Helen dress him. His eyes were not shining and bright, but sunken and flat. There was no emotion.

"Oh, Tom, why? Why did you do this? *Why*? Were you conscious?"

"Yeah, I was hot. She was cool. It happened. I dunno."

His arm was leaking green ooze down his hand. Helen cleaned it again, shuddering over the foul odor, packed it again, and wrapped it. She flashed Joy dirty looks.

Joy stuck her tongue out. She adjusted her shirt over her swimsuit and rolled her eyes.

"Is there anyone who has *not* been with you now?" asked Helen as she gave Tyrese and Alex dirty looks.

"Huh?" Joy asked.

"My God, Joy," Alex said as he shook his head.

"Me. I mean *not* me. I don't intend to either, so stay the hell away. Jeez, Tom is practically engaged," Scott raved; he was as furious as Helen.

Helen believed Scott. If he had been with Joy, too, she couldn't have taken anymore. "This is tacky, Joy. You knew better and took advantage when Tom was very ill."

Slowly, they helped Tom to his feet so they could leave. They walked toward the way down to the trail.

"He wanted to," Joy said as she shrugged.

"So? You get around *all* over!"

Joy smirked behind Helen's back and said, "You're tense 'cause you aren't getting any."

Helen snapped. That was her limit. She spun and slapped Joy's face. "Come at me. You want to go a *round*? I am telling you right now you did something immoral. You are a slut. And this time you messed up. Big. You wanna talk about me; I *will* slap you every time," Helen yelled into Joy's face.

Joy lowered her eyes.

"Good call."

"We won't tell, right?" Tom was being helped by Tyrese.

"We won't, but Bud, a secret is only safe if two people know and one is dead."

Tom sighed, "I may be dead soon. I am done."

Helen pushed forward. She dared a dinosaur to get in her way. She was a fury storm. They got water and followed the path as fast as they could with Tom injured. She encouraged Tom, and when he lagged, she begged and prodded and pushed him to keep going.

At the sled, Helen ordered Tom to get on. "I'll pull it alone if I have to, but I want to go back to camp and get Kelly to fix your arm."

Tyrese made big eyes at Scott, and they nodded.

"Joy, you're pulling, too. Get over it, and do it. We need to get back quickly."

No one objected to Helen's orders.

Straining with the loaded sled and Tom's weight, they had to work at it, but soon they were moving across the sand, and when they hit the flat part that was smoothed by the ocean waves, they zoomed over the land, moving fast. Helen felt her anger releasing as she sweated and worked. She felt better.

As soon as they saw camp, Tyrese waved as he always liked to, but no one waved back. In fact, the camp looked wrong. It wasn't tidy and organized. It was messy, and of all things, something huge was right by the water. Brown. A little blue. Big. It was Big Brown. And he was dead.

But what happened before he died? What happened to the camp?

"Run," Scott ordered.

Their sled began to move, but as they drew close, they knew things would be different, and some things would never be repaired. Joy and Tom having a dalliance was nothing compared to losing Fish. Losing Fish was nothing compared to how the camp looked.

Helen set her teeth and pulled. She ran.

Chapter 6: Day 3 At Camp

Amanda had watched the group go off earlier to explore, feeling envious that Fish was going along this time, but she had a lot to do. She had a long mental list of chores that needed to be completed around camp, and with her hand still healing, she wasn't ready for exploring the jungle. She wanted to get back to normal, at least as normal as possible, considering she was missing two fingers.

Captain Worthington sat at the fire, glad to be up and around, but he allowed Amanda to stay in leadership of the camp and watched her work, proud of her determination. He had been down for the count, but she and Fish and Joe had stepped up and assumed the burdens. He couldn't think of a better crew. A shipwreck was the nightmare of any captain, but his crewmembers had held on and protected everyone as best they could.

In the water, Stu and some of the others were fishing. The captain wished he could be out there with them in the place he loved most. He didn't blame the sea for the situation, and he didn't blame the storm, for storms were as natural as the sea, no matter how violent this one had been. Even losing his arm and watching the rest of the tragedies were acceptable as a hard part of life. It was the island he blamed. They were supposed to die at sea, get rescued, or land on a normal island; they were not supposed to land on an island inhabited by monsters that supposedly had died millions of years before. He still had no theories.

He couldn't explain what was here, but it didn't feel right to him; it felt all wrong in so many ways that he couldn't wrap his mind around the possibilities. He may have played it off as normal, but he'd never seen the yellow mist before, and he felt it was somehow to blame. Maybe he wasn't imaginative enough to figure it out.

"Durango? How are you, my friend?" Captain Mark Worthington asked.

"My head. It hurts." It was a complete thought, which was better than he managed a lot of the time.

The captain nodded.

"I know it aches, but your family needs you."

"You need to push through and help us, Durry. Vera is complaining all the time. She is using illegal drugs if you can imagine, and the so-called nurse advocates it, and Stu is an ass in general, as always. They need you to make them behave," Connie said. She scowled as Amanda handed her more tangled fishing line to unravel. "And get your crew to stop working us to death."

"Connie, Amanda is asking very little. I'm afraid the work will get far harder," the captain said. He had noticed that Connie was adjusting poorly to the situation, complaining loudly and often. Maybe Durango failed to get better because it would mean dealing with his wife.

"Durango hired you to do one thing, and you failed. We're here on this stupid island. Don't bitch at me about work when you're just sitting there," Connie said. She was angry. She loved the yacht, but she wasn't the type to do well in these conditions. Was that so hard to understand? They had failed to save the boat, and Connie was the one to suffer.

Connie dreamed of a hair appointment, a nice massage, or just a hot bath and a clean bed. She didn't expect everything to be perfect, but some bare minimums weren't too much to ask for. Didn't people understand? One stepson hardly spoke, one played hero and boss, and one was a total jerk, and her stepdaughter was a whining distraction. Of the crew, Fish was a muttering idiot, Amanda was a brute who demanded work get done, and the captain had allowed all of this to happen.

Amanda stopped in place. "With all due respect, you are not in charge anymore."

"It was our boat!"

"*Was*. Durango is in no shape to lead, and you are incapable. Fish and I have assumed authority while the captain recovers. If you think you can do any better, then I have a news flash: You can't."

Connie sniffed and replied, "You must love being in charge." If it had not been a bother, she would have stood and slapped the woman.

"Guess again. It's the last thing I ever wanted, especially under these circumstances. Please, for everyone's sake and for your family, try to help and stay calm and get along with everyone else."

"Fine. I'm reporting you when we get back." How could she say Connie was anything but calm?

"I really hope you get that chance," Amanda said. Connie's shallowness set her on edge.

"Davey...."

Davey ignored Vera. He was helping Joe, and Vera was insatiable about getting pain relief and wouldn't believe he was out of dope. He didn't tell her about what he shared with Kelly. That was his secret, and if Vera knew, she would begin begging Kelly for more. He felt sorry for Vera; she was just a kid, ten years younger than he was and scared. And spoiled. He didn't feel sorry for Connie Jones at all.

Opening a food can, Davey thought about how he once would have grimaced to see carrots but now was glad and appreciative. Joe was working on something as a treat: mangoes, carrots, coconuts, and bagged nuts they had salvaged. It would be a nice addition to dinner, but Joe claimed it was also nutritious. Davey tried to learn all he could.

That morning, Tyrese talked to Davey as they walked for a little while, still finding random items that washed up. Davey snagged a piece of a snorkel. He kept it, unsure what it could be used for but unwilling to leave it on the sand. He never knew what could be valuable now that they had so little.

Tyrese had told him, "Learn all you can, Davey. We'll survive through brains, and what will happen if we lose our nurse, cook, or leaders? Be ready to help out if you need to. You are important."

It made Davey think. He didn't want to lose anyone, but he understood that some brought more to their survival than others, and he had to pay more attention. If they lost Kelly, something Davey couldn't think about, then he could help a little. His next goal was learning what Joe did and how to do it.

"Vera, hush. Your leg looks much better. The sleep made you stronger, and you *are* healing," Kelly said.

"It hurts."

"I know it hurts, but it hurts less than day one or day two. You are going to be okay, so why don't you help Connie with the tangled line, or you can help Joe with peeling the palm, okay?"

Amanda dumped a load of palm sections beside Vera and showed her how to peel the bark away, smiling at Kelly. Surprisingly, Vera tackled the work, doing a good job and working fast. She had been spoiled her entire life, but when given orders and shown authority, she reacted as a typical teen, embracing the order and safety. Deep down, she craved the parameters.

Amanda used her hands to see better, shielding her view from the sun with her hands as visors, even if one were a clunky, bandaged visor. Vaughn, Sue, and Stu waved at her as they fished. They had good luck with the crab traps and had brought in several big fat fish for Joe to cook. There would be a time when people tired of fish, but they were lucky to have it.

Captain Worthington walked down the beach to see what Lisa was holding up. She had several squids that would make a delicious meal, and she was proud of their haul. She was grinning.

"Those are beauties," the captain called.

Stanley followed a few feet behind. He wanted to see the catch of the day. From his peripheral vision, he saw movement in the trees, but it was as if the trees were moving. The trunks looked to be moving in waves, undulating. He stopped and frowned. From the thick jungle, a huge figure emerged, racing to the water and to those who were standing on the beach. It roared and stomped as it came, sounding like tortured metal and lions, a unique noise that was terrifying.

Stanley had time to realize it was enormous, heavy- bottomed, and brown and that it had luxurious brown feathers with the tips a beautiful shade of blue. In shock, he stood in place as the three-ton animal raced over him, smashing him into the sand and snapping his lower spine.

Time stood still.

Stanley could move his head and shoulders, so he spit sand and got his face out so he could breathe, but he couldn't move. He wasn't in pain; he was numb, but he was petrified and confused. The sand grew faintly red as Stanley bled from wounds he couldn't feel. The back claws had cut his legs badly. Frustration washed over him.

The captain carried a spear that he used as a staff when he walked. He might have had only one arm, but he reacted instantly and used his one, strong arm to grip the spear and shove it at the creature, catching it in the soft belly. The wood broke as they fought. He wasn't about to let a big lizard beat him. He was sea-strong and sea-brave.

At the camp, Davey, Amanda, Joe, and Kelly grabbed weapons and advanced, yelling. Each felt afraid but angry that this creature was attacking them. Why didn't it find other dinosaurs to eat?

"Kill it. Go for the belly," Davey yelled

Infuriated and in pain, the animal twisted and contorted, slamming the captain to the ground. It would normally enjoy the stomach and soft parts of a kill, but because it was so angry, it swung around, snapped its jaws around the captain's head, bit it off, and swallowed.

Amanda sagged a little as she saw.

Those running to help screamed and yelled, unable to believe that the captain had just been killed in a very fast, but brutal way. An injury was one thing, but having one's head snapped off was not something that Kelly could fix. After all, he had been through, it was a definite shock to see him killed before his eyes. "No. Die, you dirty lizard freak," Amanda screamed. She let loose with every obscenity she could think of, and it wasn't enough. She made up words and ran them together in strings.

That had been *her* captain, her friend, and her mentor.

Lisa saw Stanley smashed into the sand and watched the captain's body fall, blood jetting from his neck. She was sure both were dead, but her focus was the enormous animal that was right in front of her. She had seen dinosaur skeletons in museums and been amazed at their size, but seeing a big live dinosaur was beyond anything she could think of. She screamed and tossed her squid at the monster, hoping it would take her offering and leave, but it watched her and advanced, cautious of another attack.

Its belly bled onto the sand but not fast enough to save Lisa. It wasn't dying, or if it were, not quickly enough. "Eat the squid," she begged it. She cried for the loss of her two friends, for her lost catch, and for herself as she felt her time was over. Despite Stu, the rest made her feel a part of the group, and Tom and Kelly made her feel special. At least she had that. She didn't want to let it go.

Sue stopped Stu and Vaughn from leaving the water, pointed to the camp, and said, "Get some weapons. Hurry."

They moved slowly, having to swim and wade a long way. They made a lot of noise and splashed, both hoping to get away unnoticed and to help those on the beach. They wanted both at the same time, but the noises didn't attract the creature; he gave them a glance and ignored the prey in the water.

The brown beast charged Lisa and knocked her down. She raised her hands and arms, but that didn't help. It ripped away her throat with a quick lunging bite, swallowing loudly as it enjoyed the warm, salty blood that sprayed, and it planned to return for the best flesh and innards; she was a big girl, and it knew, at some level, that it could feed well on her. The other two would also be good to eat.

Irritated, it spun.

Amanda had stabbed it with her weapon, a spear that had a knife on the end. It wasn't a bad wound, but it bled and hurt. As it tried to get at her, Davey ran, driving his spear into the beast's belly so far that he had to let go and back away. Both yelled as they attacked the animal, daring it to come at them.

There was a pause.

Angry, the dinosaur stopped, shocked by the attacks. What kind of prey attacked back? It was confused as it roared back. It wanted to eat what it killed, and these puny beings were stalling the plans.

Kelly couldn't get a good target, but Joe drove in a second spear, shoving it upwards. The creature bellowed and squealed. That was all it could take. It staggered. It was muddled mentally and decided to run away and leave its kills, but it felt weak with pain. Amanda and Kelly tossed their spears to Davey and Joe who bravely ran at the animal and stabbed again. Their hands went red and slippery as they stabbed and stabbed.

Both men attacked with energy and determination born of the fury of witnessing their friends' being slaughtered.

Amanda screamed as a back claw suddenly shot out and clawed her back, raking away flesh and muscle. She fell, but there wasn't another attack.

The animal took a few more breaths, roared weakly, and thumped over, dead. It was almost surreal to see it die all at once. Stu, Vaughn, and Sue ran over, ready to fight, but it was all over. It felt anticlimactic to them, as well.

"Get Stanley back to camp," Stu ordered.

Davey and Joe went to get Stanley, having to drag the man back. Stanley wailed and said he was unable to feel anything beneath his nipple line. Kelly ran alongside, ready to do her work.

Stu picked up Amanda in his arms and carried her back while she shivered and cried out with pain. His arms and chest became drenched in gore as he carried her, telling her she would be fine and muttering the same few sentences over and over, unable to think clearly.

Vaughn looked at Sue and asked, "What is it?"

"I have no idea. Something unknown." She stared at the body of the dead dinosaur. "We may be the first to know of this kind. I wish we had never seen it. Asshole dinosaur, I hate it."

"What about Lisa?" asked Vaughn who was troubled. The attack had been unexpected and gruesome. How had this happened when a few minutes before there had been peace on the beach? It was unfair after everything they had suffered.

Sue felt for a pulse, despite the blood all over the sand, and shook her head. She had trouble even finding a place to feel in the carnage of Lisa's neck. "At least it was fast." She picked up the squid for reasons she didn't understand and carried them with her. The captain's headless body lay in the sand.

Vaughn leaned over and vomited. Sue nodded and patted his back. She gagged several times as well.

At the camp close to the slaughter, Kelly tossed things all over the sand, trying to determine who to treat first. "Davey...Stanley. Do what you can." She told Stu to lay Amanda face down on a mat, and she yelled orders. Pamela gathered everything Kelly demanded, and Vera painfully crawled over to pat Amanda's hand.

Vera was sorry now that she had argued with Amanda, but more than that, she was aware that some time, this might be her, and she needed to stay on everyone's good side. Her leg kept her from having to be a dinosaur fighter for now, but she knew that had she been uninjured, she might have been the one to be ripped up as Amanda was.

Kelly took a deep breath.

Using scissors, she removed the rest of Amanda's shirt and looked at the injury. Muscles and fat showed, and blood was pouring out. "Oh, Amanda, what can I do?"

Kelly knew the wound was filthy from the claw. There would be bacteria from feces and rotten food embedded, yet cleaning it seemed futile and torture. Still, she thought of Fish and set her jaw. "Joe, heat metal…knives…whatever you have…even the bottom of a pot. I need things white hot. Give me that alcohol."

"No," Amanda wailed, knowing what was coming, "don't do it, Kelly; I'll be okay."

Kelly wiped away tears and set her jaw. "I hope you forgive me one day."

Amanda screamed and twisted around, fighting as Kelly poured the liquid onto the wounds and scrubbed them clean. Stu and Vaughn held her in place and were nearly bucked away several times. The agony had to be unreal. Vaughn was pale as he did his job but reeled with the agony he heard in Amanda's screams.

Kelly's fingers felt numb, but she dug in her stash and slid a pill into Amanda's mouth. "Swallow, and don't ask what this is or who gave it to me."

Amanda weakly did as she was told, but whispered, "Kelly, I can't take any more. Please, stop." She thought she would rather die than to suffer this, and as much as Kelly wanted to help, the pain was far too much to stand.

"Nope. Listen, you are going to do this. Smoke this. Stu, hold it. It may take the edge off." Kelly lit a marijuana cigarette and handed it to Stu, who looked shocked but nodded. In her wildest dreams, Kelly never imagined giving a patient illegal drugs, but she just had administered two. The rules had changed. She and Stu traded glances and had a rare understanding between them.

Joe had tears in his eyes, but he pushed past Kelly and set a red hot knife on the bloodiest part of Amanda's back the second she finished her cigarette. He didn't ask or hesitate, just did what was needed.

Amanda bucked and screeched.

Kelly told herself it was better than without the drugs. "Again." Kelly dimly wished she, as the nurse, could have some drugs, too. "Doctor, that's a lot of whiskey. Should I drink that much? Nah. That's mine. Did you want some, too?"

"Kelly?" Stu asked.

"Just some medical humor."

Pamela passed Joe another glowing knife that Joe laid sideways again on the worst of the injury, searing the flesh, killing the germs, and sealing the blood vessels. Amanda passed out, but her body jerked and twitched each time they repeated the process. Five times, they used fire to burn her skin and stop the bleeding. It was of no help or consolation, but everyone was weeping as he treated Amanda.

"The bleeding is better. It has almost stopped except for a few spots. I am going to stitch those." Kelly worked meticulously, pretending this was normal, but inwardly cringing as she sewed spots that were next to burned, charred flesh. "Doctor, is this gonna hurt? Nah. Not a bit; oh, you meant would it hurt *you*?" Kelly talked to herself, trying to keep from thinking about what she had just done to poor Amanda.

Using coconut water mixed with rum, she cleaned Amanda's back.

When she was finished, she asked them to move Amanda close to the fire to stay warm and said that was all she could do. She left the wounds uncovered. Tears streaked her face although she didn't know it. She had cried all the way through her make-shift surgery.

"Davey? How is Stanley?"

"Not good. I cleaned his cuts, but his back is broken, Kelly. He...his bowels released." Davey explained the foul odor. He cleaned Stanley, and they moved him next to the fire as well. He shook his head at Kelly; he didn't think Stanley had a chance of survival.

She shook her head as she looked at Amanda.

"Lisa, the captain...." Vera stared into space, shaking. She didn't even complain that Kelly had a stash of pot. Everyone around her was dead or dying, and her own father was a shell of a man.

Durango had not reacted at all during the attack. He looked at the sea.

Down the beach, Tyrese waved as they brought the sled back to camp. No one waved back. They didn't have the energy.

Chapter 7: Nightfall, Day Three

Joy, Scott, Helen, Tyrese, and Alex dragged the sled and Tom into camp and fell on their butts, exhausted. They saw the captain's body lying headless. They saw the blood and Lisa's body by the water. They saw the big brown dinosaur.

All of that was overwhelming.

Scott told the rest about losing Fish and finding the remains of other people and then waited to hear what had happened. He talked fast and said he would explain in detail later. The camp smelled of feces and burned flesh.

Sue gave a recount of the attack, but the events were easy to figure out by looking at the bodies on the beach. "At least the Big Brown is dead."

"Ummmph," Alex made a noise.

"He *is* dead. They killed the bastard. They were heroes."

"Yeah, she's dead. She's very dead, true, but...." Alex rubbed his head and walked back to the dinosaur and then returned, sitting down again to rub his head. He looked upset and perplexed as he thought and searched his brain for answers.

"We don't have to worry about it anymore, I mean," Sue said. She was confused over Alex's reaction. He was as fascinated with dinosaurs as she was, and despite the circumstances, he was curious, but now he acted strange.

"She's very feathered. She's big but *not* as *big*; she has a lot of feathers. She...." Alex took a deep breath and said, "That *isn't* Big Brown."

"Yes, it is. It's brown and has feathers, and it's dead now," Stu said. He felt dread creeping into his stomach with a lump of anxiety.

"No, she looks like Big Brown, but she is far more feathered, and Big Brown is male. Go look at her belly and the remains of her brood. They must have live births because there are two dead babies I can see in that mess of her stomach. That is absolutely not Big Brown." Alex spat the words out with a raised voice, sick with having to relate the information. It was as if it were his fault that this was the wrong dinosaur. It was not the *wrong* one, really, but it was *another* one. He didn't like that he knew it. He really didn't like saying it. And mostly, he hated being right.

"What does that mean?" Stu asked.

"Alex," Sue said. She saw that his eyes were full of fear. "You killed Big Brown's mate. There is a bigger one out there, and I suspect when he figures this out, he is going to be furious. I mean if they are that advanced and can feel emotions, some animals get pissed off when their mates are killed."

"Another one?" Vera asked.

Alex nodded.

Helen said, "He's right. I am sure that isn't Big Brown. It looks like him, but it isn't. Kelly, Tom is in trouble."

Kelly had been so busy that when she saw Tom, she didn't understand that he was on the sled and very sick. She wanted to yell at him for not having his arm treated earlier, and she knew he shouldn't have gone out, but all that was useless now. She looked at his arm and nodded and murmured as he spoke.

"I didn't know what to do except drain it and use what we had. We hurried back."

"You did what you could," Kelly said, "and now we have to be stronger."

"I...Fish was gone, he...." Helen stammered, but she and Kelly knew what Fish would have done. It made Helen very afraid. More than ever, they needed Fish.

Quietly, Kelly nodded and walked around the camp, whispering and watching surreptitiously as people did her bidding. She understood only too well how much they needed Fish.

Joe had been experimenting, cutting away a bit of the dinosaur, cooking it well, and tasting it. He gave Vera a bite, and though she scowled, she nodded approval. Davey tried it and found it to taste somewhere between chicken and alligator. *Everything tastes like chicken.* The way Joe cooked it well done and spiced it up made it very good.

"I'll need help, but I am gonna carve that thing into steaks, and we'll eat fine. I can smoke some of the meat for later. It won't go to waste."

"Then, we will need to haul the body out to sea so we don't attract predators. We have to hurry," Vaughn said.

Stu patted his younger brother for thinking ahead.

Joe readied his utensils, setting the machete in the fire; it was the only one they had, and a fluke to have found it; he needed it. Tyrese stood close and stretched his big, muscular arms. He was nervous with sudden energy and had to stretch and twist to release tension.

Stu unwrapped a length of rope that he handed to Vaughn. He went to Tom and asked, "How are you doing?"

"Uhhh. Hurts. Doing fine."

"Yeah? Good. Tom, you're a good brother. I think you're the best of the family. You got all the good traits, and we got what was left."

"Huh?"

"You're a good man, Tom," was all Stu said.

Scott hugged Helen, and they walked over to Kelly who unwrapped Tom's arm again to check it. The injury had gone blackish and was pouring green ooze.

Fish was an amazing fellow, wasn't he?" Kelly said. "I will miss him so much. He was a true hero in all ways." She paused and looked up. "*Now.*"

Vaughn tied Tom's legs with the rope, wrapping the rope over and around as if making a mummy. He then sat on Tom's legs. At the same time, Stu grabbed Tom in a bear hug that Scott joined.

"Wha...." Tom's head snapped around. What was happening?

Joe grabbed Tom's injured arm and held it down with his knees, causing terrible pain. Tom yelped. He knew as Kelly and Helen leaned over him. "No, Oh, hell, no. I'll kill you fuckers, no. Please. No." He sobbed between threats.

Tyrese grabbed the mini-machete, didn't hesitate, swung it up, and slammed it down onto Tom's arm, right below the shoulder where the flesh was healthy. All of it went as planned. Everyone had done as Kelly demanded.

Tom roared.

Tyrese was strong, but the circumstances were poor, and he had to hit the arm two more times to sever it. Each time, he felt sick and wanted to stop and scream, but he was given a job, and he would see it done. He was chosen because he was very strong, and this was his chore; he had to finish.

"Move him. Now," Kelly yelled. Scott and Stu yanked Tom closer to the fire where Joe had arranged red coals for this purpose.

Tom's eyes rolled back as he screamed, and he stopped making noise and just jerked wildly, but they held his stump to the coals until it was black and crisp. There were pops and soft *plinks* as the stump seared.

"Okay, move him back," said Kelly, and with Helen's help, she checked to be sure the bleeding was stopped. If it wasn't, they'd have to use a hot blade like they had used on Amanda. Kelly felt that she and Joe were cooking their friends and almost giggled.

"Kelly," Helen said, "come on." She saw Kelly beginning to lose her composure. 'Don't make me slap you. Get it together."

"She does slap," Joy hissed.

Kelly nodded.

They bathed the stump, and Kelly saw that the bleeding was only slight. She hoped she had gotten the poisoned arm off before it killed Tom, and she saw that there were no streaks that far up. After slathering it in cream, Kelly and Helen wrapped the stump.

Some worked to bury the captain and Lisa at sea like they had buried others, while others stood guard. Someone removed the severed arm. Joe, Sue, and Davey worked to carve the dinosaur into steaks, and Vera, Joy, and Pamela wrapped them carefully and worked quietly.

Tom received the last hidden doses of antibiotics; Kelly had two more vials, and both would be his.

Helen straightened and organized the camp. She liked the time alone as she worked. When the captain was incapacitated, Fish and Amanda took over because they were crew. Fish was dead, and Amanda was in bad shape; she could be dismissed. Durango, the owner of the boat, was unwell and didn't feel as if he would ever recover. Brain injury. That left the leadership to Tom, the oldest of the sons. He was lying somewhere between life and death and couldn't be looked at to lead them.

In a perfect world, they would need no leader and would function as a hive, working together and surviving, but they weren't bees. She giggled to herself. And stopped. Had anyone noticed? No. She could go back to her thinking.

Who was next in line? Technically, it was Stu. He had been easier to deal with lately and was very strong when needed. He was a ready, brave fighter, smart, and a tireless worker, but what would happen to him and his big ego if he were put in as the group leader?

Who else?

Kelly was a good leader, but she was far too busy. People would not follow her since her mind was on saving the wounded. Not Davey, or Vaughn, or Joe. They weren't the types. Pamela, Vera, Joy, and Connie were noes.

Sue was strong, but she wasn't tough enough, not quite. She could in a pinch, maybe. That left four possibilities: Scott, Alex, Tyrese, and her. Of them, who could stand up to Stu and take his rightful leadership? She couldn't because she was a female, and he was a sexist.

Alex was the smartest, but he was a weaker fighter. Scott was smart and brave, but he held back. Tyrese was brave, self-assured, and a fighter.

Helen decided she would speak to the others and see if they would push for Tyrese to lead. It was only logical.

After the camp was clean, the men hacked up the dinosaur carcass and floated it far away. They were terrified of being attacked as the sun began sinking, but nothing happened, and the scene of the battle was soon cleaned away. Each person was exhausted past anything he could imagine, and Davey gave them a lot of water and coconut water.

A small storm was coming, and they stowed everything away, getting ready. They'd all have to sleep in the wreck and hope the fire stayed going and kept the monsters away.

At first, everyone, except Davey and Vera who had tried the dinosaur steaks, was hesitant to try the huge slabs of meat. The char on them made them glance at Amanda and Tom and turn their stomachs a little. One by one they tried the meat, finding it tender and delicious. It filled their stomachs fully, something soups and stews and crab legs never did. There were squids, eel, and the carrot-coconut dish that Joe had made. They ate past being full, so much that they stuffed themselves, but they needed the calories after everything they had been through. Only Connie refused the main course; she would eat only the eel.

"I'll smoke the rest in the morning after we have had more to eat," Joe said. He helped set up buckets for rainwater.

In the wreckage, some slept close together, and some went off alone or in pairs. Some snickered as Joy slept alone. She was strangely quiet.

Stu and Tyrese stayed near the entrance with Joe, weapons close at hand.

Helen, under blankets with Scott, reached up and kissed him and asked, 'Is that okay?" He kissed her back so thoroughly that it was clear it was more than okay. Still nervous, scared, and worried, they clung to one another, and in their corner and as quietly as possible with slow movements, Scott lost his shyness and explored Helen's body gently, making her bite her lips often. They made love several times until they were tired and satiated physically and emotionally.

"Helen."

"Umm?" She looked into his pretty green eyes and wished they could stay this way.

"You don't have to say anything, but I need to. I…I love you. I think I have for a while now."

She smiled and replied, "I love you, too. It scares me because I am far more worried about your staying safe. I can't lose you now that I found you."

"I know. I will worry about you all the time. But I'll protect you. It's real; I really love you."

She lay her head on his shoulder and said, "It's all I need."

Their conversation balanced another one across the wreckage as Tom awoke and spoke to Kelly. His voice was weak and dull as he said, "I told you no. I begged."

"I had no choice. I had to save your life."

"You saw the captain with one arm, die. I said no. I meant no."

"It wasn't your choice anymore. I saved you."

Tom let the tears flow. With the memory of the pure torture and pain, he preferred to be dead. He wanted to die. He ate the pills Kelly gave him and drank the water. He didn't care to argue. "I was going to propose at the end of the cruise. I was going to ask for you to marry me."

"That's sweet." Kelly thought of that and how romantic it would have been. She would have said yes, and they would have planned a huge ceremony, been married, had a few children, and either lived happily ever after or divorced after a few years, just like Tom's parents. The idea was beautiful even if it were all over.

"I'm not sure I know you. I don't know if I can or want to get to know who you are. You've changed. You don't have the same smile."

Kelly thought that over. "I don't feel much like smiling lately. Okay. I think you're right. I'm not sure who I am, either. It's okay."

"I'm angry with you. I'm not sure I hate you, but I don't like you, Kelly."

"Okay," She gulped away the pain of hearing that, but it was about to get worse.

"You are too set in your own ways of thinking and can't hear anyone else speaking or accept other ideas. It isn't pretty, Kelly. I need something. Someone's got to stay by me and make sure I'm okay, right?"

"I'm here."

"Yeah. I don't want to see you or talk to you. Maybe not for a while. Can you send Joy?"

"Joy?" asked Kelly who felt as if she were slapped.

"Thank you. Yes, Joy," said Tom, enjoying the stinging barb he dealt Kelly.

Kelly got up and took her covers. She went over and saw Joy was awake. "Trade places. I want this place alone, and Tom is asking for you. He's not fond of me right now."

"Okay. You *did* take off his arm."

"To save his life!"

"Well, yeah but…."

Kelly narrowed her tired eyes and asked, "Would you have let him die?"

"I guess. I wouldn't have taken off his arm, though. That was…well…it's over, but it wasn't right since he told you no."

Kelly motioned her away and said, "Go. Go sit with him. He needs sips of water, and if he bleeds again, come wake me." Kelly rolled into her covers and cried until she fell asleep. Her choices were bad; in fact, all of them were bad.

Hard sheets of rain fell, and thunder rolled ominously, yet there was little wind. It was a mild thunderstorm, but it reminded them of the bad storm that ruined the boat and sent them to this hell-on-earth. Hearing the thunder, several shivered and shook with dread. Bad memories might never be erased; certainly, they couldn't as long as they were castaways on an island covered in monsters.

While most slept and the early risers began the work of starting the fire blazing and setting the camp back to rights, a figure slipped next to Stanley and ran a razor across his throat and stepped out of the blood pool. The figure walked close to Amanda, but she mumbled in her sleep and was passed over for death. Vera was better and hardly given a glance. The figure studied Pamela but let her live. Durango Jones was last. The killer planned to slice Durango's throat and let him go on, but more people were awakening.

The chance was lost. For this night.

The sun was rising on a new day.

Chapter 8: Day Four

Kelly, Helen, Tyrese, and Scott prepared Stanley's body and had the others send him into the sea for a burial. Kelly asked them not to share the cause of death, but it was clear someone cut his throat. Maybe it was a merciful action. Maybe it was selfish in killing the weakest link. It was impossible to know.

The four of them looked at everyone suspiciously, and even the four looked at one another the same way. Anyone could be the killer. There had been forty aboard the boat several days ago, watching the yellow and purple storm roll in. Now, they were down to seventeen with two in bad shape and three in serious condition. The odds were getting poorer.

Kelly was hoping that the three she chose to trust were the right ones to believe in. She figured they wondered the same about her. She had cooked Amanda's back and cut off Tom's arm. She was like an angel of torture and how close to that was an angel of mercy? In her mind, they were far apart.

"We have plenty of water. No need to scout, right?" Kelly asked.

Helen pushed a little and asked, "What do you think, T?"

Tyrese said, "I would like to check some other trails and mull over the events that were written about in the diary."

Helen waved the diary in the air. As they ate, she summarized the story, "There was a storm. The plane crashed in the trees, and about a fifth of the passengers were killed outright or died shortly thereafter of injuries. After that, they met the dinosaurs; they called them *Shorty, Stinky, Fat Purple, Big Teeth,* and *Little Chickens* although sometimes they used the real, scientific names. It was a man who wrote that part. His name was Jim. He says that *compys are really delicious, better than meat eaters.*

"See?" Connie said with a sniff, "the eel was lovely."

"Thank you, Miss Connie," Joe grinned.

"Anyway, they had food and water, and they lived in the wreckage, just like we do. Some decided that was wrong and that if they were stuck there, they could do better. That's when about three-fourths packed their share and went to live in the caves. They stayed in touch. For some reason, half of the cave group: teens, pre-teens, and children all the way down to six years old became dissatisfied within a week. They grabbed *their* supplies and left, sneaking out one night. The parents tried to get them back, but the group of young people threatened the parents and refused."

"*Lord of the Flies*?" Tyrese quipped.

"I know. Get this. The parents thought the pool of water that the kids swam in and drank from was the cause of the problems with the young people. The parents said the water tasted horrible, but the kids drank it. Jim surmised that natural steroids or something else were in the water because the kids started growing faster, and breasts were developing on the six-year-old, and they were getting aggressive and were always hungry. He said that explained why the dinosaurs were overly muscular and aggressive as well. That's his theory."

Alex shrugged and said, "Or dinos are just aggressive in general?"

"*True.* What happened after that?" Sue asked.

"They didn't know where most of the kids went to live, but some wanted their babies back, so there were fights. Some went to search and never returned. The rest stayed, and they had less and less contact with the people in the plane. They seemed to be having more attacks from dinosaurs, and it ended with Jim's saying that seven of them, a third even after the kids left, were going to kill the Utahraptor's leaders if they could. They would be back."

"Is that all?"

"That's it. It sounds as if they had internal problems and kid problems....well...and dinosaur problems."

"If that water is real, it isn't a magic fountain but some water that lies in pools where there are minerals and mosses that water leeches out. You can get enzymes, steroid-like stuff, just weird chemicals, but I want a big bottle of it," Kelly said. Davey and Alex nodded.

"Why?" Helen asked.

"We have nothing to lose. If it's real, it could help Tom, Amanda, and maybe Durango. It's worth a shot. Don't call it a fairy tale. It may be simple science...rocks and chemicals...very normal stuff that can help," said Kelly, hoping they would agree.

"Places that are called magical usually are only filled with common nutrients or things our bodies need," Alex said. "If people with leg cramps found a pool of water rich in quinine and potassium, they would think it was a miracle; those things simply stop leg pain. Logical."

Helen turned to Tyrese and asked, "Who is going on this trip?"

"You, Scott, Alex, me," said Tyrese and then paused, "Kelly, you hold tough. Joe and Stu? You have it okay?"

"I have it," Stu called. He hoped that was true. In his head, he decided that they would be very careful and fight if needed, but no one was going to die on his watch. Then, he wondered about Stanley. He turned to Kelly and asked, "What happened to Stan? Really?"

She sighed and said, "Really, a big bad monster stomped him. He died. That's all." She watched the others leave, hoping the pool of water was there and could be located. It might help.

The other four left with the sled and went to the familiar trail. Helen gave what she thought were directions to where the mysterious water would be. It wasn't far from the cave and was on the way to where the plane might be.

Alex laughed as soon as he saw the pool and knew this was the one. "I think maybe there are rocks and soil full of steroids and under the water, but look at that? Suma trees and their roots go down into the pool. They are loaded with steroids. See those beans?"

"Can we eat them?"

Alex laughed and said, "We'll pick every one right now so we get them in our packs safely. Fava beans. They contain steroids, too.

This pool must be thick with them." Shockingly, Alex, with no embarrassment, stripped down and went into the pool, a pretty sky blue if the pool had been clear, but it was almost a foggy, white-blue. He didn't yell or complain but moved around and said, "It feels wonderful." After bathing in the sea water, he added, "This is nice, and it feels soothing." He took a gulp, scaring them. "Not great. Not bad." He gulped a few more times and began gathering fava beans for his bag.

"Come on," said Scott as he helped undress Helen who blushed furiously, but she followed him in and found the water delicious-feeling. She filled a bottle for Kelly and then picked beans. "So it's natural?"

"Very, I think it may be extremely condensed, and there may be other things in this pool, but it isn't so weird to find, not as weird as discovering dinosaurs on an island," Alex said, "and it's unexpected, yes, but we are due a miracle."

Tyrese gave in and joined them. In a few minutes, he laughed and said, "Am crazy, but I swear my cuts and scrapes feel better, and my broken fingers aren't aching. Power of suggestion."

Helen looked over and said, "T, your scrapes do look better. No kidding. Is that possible?"

Alex shook his head and answered, "Nope, not possible, not that fast. But since when are dinosaurs possible?"

"They aren't."

"Exactly. We can pretend all we want, but face it, no island in a busy part of the sea is going to be undiscovered. If we were somewhere else...maybe...but come on, this place would have been found. Besides that, our boat wrecked. People know. Don't you think people are searching? But we've never seen a plane looking for us."

"What does that mean?" Scott asked.

"We don't talk about it, but we know. This isn't right. We would have been found, or at least, we would have seen airplanes over head. Nothing. There is no way this place can be here, yet it is. I thought maybe we died, and this was a dream I was having, but I don't think so."

"Unless we're having the same dream," said Helen who laughed and then asked, "but am I in yours or are you in mine?"

Alex agreed, "Exactly, Helen. It's real, but it isn't right. It's impossible. On the other hand, some real rules apply. There are dinosaurs, and they can kill, but they can also be killed. This pool makes sense, somewhat on a scientific level, but what are the chances it would be here and be found so easily?"

"I agree," Tyrese said.

"And if it exists, despite the odds, why can't it help heal because that is scientific, but not really possible," Scott summarized.

"Therefore, my hand feels better," said Tyrese as he laughed. "And scrapes are better, yet nothing else exactly makes sense here on this island. Do you think, I mean…did we go somewhere else. Alex?"

"I would say no, but honestly I don't know at all. I don't think our brains are capable of understanding what happened to us or where we are, but it isn't the place we knew before. I hope we can get back to our place…."

Helen said quietly, "I don't think we can. I think we are here and have to accept it. You know what I thought of? Yeah, we landed on a place with dinosaurs, maybe in another time, for all we know, or another plane of reality, who knows, but my point is what if we had landed somewhere worse?"

"Worse?" Scott asked. He was digesting the information and was unsure what he believed. It was like God: God either *was* or was *not* and certainly didn't depend on Scott's belief to exist. In this situation, Scott's opinion didn't matter, either; they were here, among living relics that were real, and the way they got here was not dependent on *his* beliefs.

Helen went on, "I mean, we don't understand, and I doubt we ever will, really. But I was thinking that if we came to be here with of all things, dinosaurs, where is it we could have landed? What if another small island is filled with hot lava and man-eating fire squid? Stop laughing."

They all laughed anyway, and she grinned.

Alex sobered and agreed, "I think that's true. Not the lava squid, maybe, but we don't know what could be here in this universe."

"I think we didn't switch universes," Scott said, "maybe this is hell."

"You believe in hell but not a different universe?" Tyrese asked, amused.

"I think, I mean, I don't know, and it doesn't matter what I think. We're here. I have a bad feeling that it's as if you are hinting that there won't be a rescue, and if we had a magic boat and sailed away, there might not be a better place."

"Depressing."

Alex nodded at Tyrese and said, "That's why I haven't said anything but to you guys. I think a few may be catching on. Not sure. But this turned into a long discussion about everything else when I wanted to say this pool is strange and impossible, but I think we can expect the impossible to be real sometimes."

They finished picking the beans, and Helen dug up the Suma roots for Kelly. Helen had felt tired this morning, but now, the exhaustion was gone. Maybe it was magic, here. She saw the others were more energetic.

Tyrese liked the water enough that he drank a lot and ate the beans.

They hated to leave and understood how the children became addicted. They had more energy and felt clean, and small aches and cuts were no longer stinging. Helen pulled her long, dark hair back and let it stay wet. Kelly was right, and they were excited to tell her.

First, they went in the direction they thought the plane was.

It wasn't difficult to find because of the trails. But as she figured out the sketchy directions, they found what they were seeking. There it was.

Slightly crumpled, the plane sat at an angle to the ground, and the angle of the wing made a gentle slope up to an emergency door. Scott pegged a few stones at the plane and waited. It was likely there was no one there, just like the cave. In seconds, a face appeared at a window. A woman looked out and then closed the shade again.

"Did you see that? There's someone here," said Helen who was excited and nervous.

"They will be as scared of us as we are of them. They don't expect to see anyone. Same as us," Tyrese warned.

It took several minutes, but the door opened, and a man looked out. "I am air marshal of the plane. Who are you, why are you here, and what are you seeking? How did you come to be here?" he asked, sounding strong and stern.

"We were on a yacht in a storm and shipwrecked four days ago. We have lost almost half our people to the injuries in the wreck and from the monsters. We are the same as you...lost here. We found you through a diary one of your people wrote and kept in a cave. His name was Jim. We seek answers to this place since we are newcomers," Tyrese called.

"How fairs Jim?"

"There was no one in the cave. We found a few remains in a Utahraptor nest. It looks as if they have been gone a long time from the cave. Months."

The man leaned back to speak and then nodded and asked, "And the kids?"

"We have seen no children. No signs of them."

"Come up. If you try to rob us, we'll fight back."

"We have no intention of robbing anyone," Tyrese said.

The plane was tidy and shadowy. They sat across from the man, who said he was Lynn, the leader or the marshal. There were four other men and five women, and they were told another woman was in the other section. "She's dying. She is trying to give birth, and the baby won't come, and she's bleeding to death. Her name is Shelly."

"Lynn, we have a real nurse at our camp. If we took Shelly there, she might could be saved." Tyrese shared some dried fish with them, some peanuts in a package, and a few fava beans." He grinned at Helen over the last offering.

"We don't leave here. It isn't safe; we barely forage."

"And you're thin and pale," Helen said honestly. How many from your group have died? Half? More than half? Two-thirds?" She thought that was right when Marshal Lynn dropped his eyes.

"You could die with us, too, but you'd die with sunshine on your faces and fresh fish and vegetables and fruit in your bellies," said Scott; he was being honest.

"Man can't live in caves and go backwards. We can't devolve the children...."

"We figured out what caused it. Too much of a good thing. And I agree caves aren't a good place to run to. For all that, Jim's group must not have survived. The caves weren't the answer."

Lynn nodded at Helen.

"Who leads you?" a woman named Lilly asked.

"Tyrese," Helen said. Alex and Scott, whom she had already spoken to, nodded. Tyrese was surprised but nodded, too.

"I try, but there are ones who would want to lead; it's a slippery slope."

"That's why Jim left. He was a steward and thought that gave him power. I was an air marshal, all out of bullets."

Helen heard more in Lynn's voice. She knew he had tried to lead, had been left, and had felt hopeless now that his gun was useless. The lines on his face were from worry and fear. These people were a glimpse into her future, possibly. Their group could separate. All that they had better was that they were on the beach and well fed and had been here only a little while.

Who were they to give advice to those who had survived a longer time here? But to see people starving and afraid was more than Helen could stand. She thought Amanda and Fish would have led them to help these people.

Tyrese was a leader, after all. He said, "We have some injured in the wreck. We have some who were injured in attacks by the monsters, but we have a roomy camp. If you just wish to visit, we could learn more about your experiences and tell you ours. I promise dino steaks, eel, crab, oysters, squid, fresh fish, fruits, vegetables, and a real, certified nurse. We would welcome you, arshal, and treat you as an equal to us."

Helen knew Tyrese was the perfect choice. He was very political, after all. There was a reason they had been attacked and then found the cave and the diary that led them here. There was always a purpose even if it weren't always clear at first. A devout Catholic, Helen believed in purposes and felt there had to be a bigger plan, even if she hated it so far and questioned it.

Lynn looked at all the faces in the plane, and asked, "How can we get Shelly there?"

"You have some litter here, right? Something from the plane? Once we get to the beach, we have a sled."

"She'll die for sure if we don't try," Lilly said.

"What if the children see an attack? The creatures carry people away, and those never return," a woman said, shaking.

"If they attack, we'll fight them. If they are a threat, I'll get people and go clean them out once and for all," Tyrese declared.

"They won't win."

"It's what we've prayed for: someone to come and take them out so we can live peacefully in the place without fear," a man whispered.

Air Marshal Lynn stood. That made up his mind, and he said, "Take your bedrolls and what you can carry on your backs. Your hands are for weapons. RJ and Shona, you get Shelly on the litter, wrap her well, and then get her down. We'll help."

It wasn't easy, and they almost dropped Shelly several times. On the trail, Helen got Shelly to eat a few fava beans and some sea grapes and to drink the mysterious water. She placed clean rags that were soaked in the water against Shelly's privates, hoping the water was a little magical.

Marshal Lynn leaned over to Helen and said, "Thank you."

They followed the trails, showing new ones to the new group. They had impressive weapons, sharp spears, and deadly spikes. Nothing and no one approached them. They settled Shelly's litter onto the sled, and this time, the new people did all the pulling, and they made good time.

Helen noticed she still wasn't tired, and she liked that.

When they saw the camp this time, it looked normal and busy, well-guarded, and tidy again. Unfortunately, the big carcass of the Big Brown they had killed was washed up way down the beach, and they could see medium-sized and little predators gorging on the rotting flesh. At least it was a long way down the beach where it was barely visible.

"See what washed up again? Yuk," Stu said as he walked over. He was stunned at seeing new faces but was curious. What stories did these skinny people have to tell?

Everyone was welcomed and tentatively sat down to talk. Any worries were dispelled as Joe served lunch: scallops, oysters, and crab in a purslane salad, and dinosaur steaks topped with crispy, fresh fish. The new comers' stomachs had shrunk with near starvation, but they ate all they could and actually laughed and relaxed.

Helen whispered to Kelly and caught her up on what Alex had explained about natural steroids and added that they thought there were minerals as well. "Kelly, I am not crazy. Our smaller cuts healed right then."

Kelly examined Shelly who was terrified and found the bleeding was almost stopped. "Get her more of those beans and water…just a little, and I'm going to clean her well with the water. It may be that the stuff is just saturated with steroids."

Helen nodded and added, "Vera, Tom, Durango, Pamela, Amanda, maybe it will work for all of you."

"Well, it sure as hell can't hurt. This stuff clots blood almost instantly, too. Helen, you are a genius and life saver!"

Kelly finally went to eat her meal and smiled broadly at Air Marshal Lynn. "The bleeding has stopped, and her labor is very normal now. The baby seems to be fine so far. It's still alive. She is worn out and weak, so we'll have to see how she does."

There were cheers all around, and of all things, the air marshal went to his knees before Kelly and looked up at her and said, "You are an angel."

"No way, Helen helped the most. Shelly is still worn out, and it will be a hard delivery, but she seems far better, and I am going to take her some food and water as soon as I finish my lunch."

"May I do it and see her?" he asked as his grey eyes kit up with hope.

"Why sure, Marshal."

As soon as they finished eating, Helena and Kelly went to bathe Amanda's back and hand while Alex gave her the water to drink. Jelly bathed Durango's head, and Helen gave him water. They did the same for Vera's legs and got her to eat fava beans, and Kelly mashed up Suma root and packed it on the wound. They went to Pamela and bathed her poor face. Then, they went to Tom, fed him the beans, gave him water, and bathed his stump before bandaging it with the Suma root. But Kelly frowned.

"What?"

"My hands were raw from all the scrubbing, and the skin was cracked. Look. They aren't healed, but they look better, Helen."

"It works, doesn't it?"

"Oh, I hope it does."

The new people were not ones to sit around. Some helped fish, enjoying it and laughing; others walked guard duty with weapons and looked deadly; and others helped with cooking or washing. Other than having to learn new names, it was if they had always been with the original group. Their moods had changed at once.

Over hearty dino and vegetable stew, the new comers had explained what had happened to them.

Four months before, their plane hit a yellow fog (Stu used this to say he had told them so) and lost altitude. Only because the pilot was gifted and caught a perfect wind, did he manage to keep the plane in the air and stable so that they glided into the trees. But they glided in much too fast, however, and the pilot and copilot and everyone in first class were crushed and torn apart. Many others were hit by flying objects that bounced around the cabin, there was one heart attack victim, and a fourth of the passengers were killed in the crash.

"We thought help would come. We waited. I didn't understand," Air Marshal Lynn said.

"We were the same way," Scott told them, "and we waited and asked each other why someone hadn't come; it was the hardest part. We felt...."

"Forgotten," Alex supplied.

"We buried all of them and figured out fairly fast that we were on a terrible island filled with monsters. We lost two more to the creatures. It seemed impossible, but it was real," Shona said, "and we didn't understand. No one came, and we were all alone. A week passed."

"Very upsetting," said Alex as he nodded.

"We explored a little. Jim decided he was in charge and that we would move to the caves, but the air marshal appealed to us, saying that we couldn't devolve and that the plane was well built and very safe. We debated for weeks. If not for the plane, we would have been killed."

"The plane saved you, I think," Alex said, "it gave you a strong, sturdy shelter. Seems they should have listened to an air marshal. We had no cops with us, nothing like that. Jim made a mistake, but I guess he thought he was in charge?"

"He did. I get that, but he was wrong about caves; the little ones could get into caves, but they never got into the plane."

"I shot a few monsters," the air marshal said, "and we ate them."

"Jim took his followers and all the children, theirs, and those who had been orphaned when their parents died in the crash, and left for the caves. We stayed in touch," said Shona, shivering, "but it didn't get better. None of us knew how to survive in this kind of situation, and it had been a long time since the crash. Of those who had been hurt, half died."

"And then Jim sent word to us about the children. It felt as if everything were over and that we'd fought a battle for nothing," Marshal said.

"What happened?" Scott asked.

Air Marshal Lynn explained that there was a pool of water. All of them thought it had certain excellent properties and helped many of the wounded recover. People were less tired and felt stronger.

"We know that pool," Tyrese said.

"The kids and teens began to stay in it all the time, we heard. They were in all day and half the night. They quickly reached sexual maturity, but they became aggressive and combative. They became too strong and threatened Jim's group: their parents. Only the smallest children were safe. It must be an evil pool of water," Bobby said.

Kelly shook her head and said, "No, It isn't at all. It's very natural but unusual. Minerals are in the water, and two plants live there that add steroids to the water. Used as a medicine *only,* the water and plants are like a miracle drug. It's what I used to save Shelly because she and the baby were a few hours from certain death."

"*That* water?" asked Marshal Lynn who looked worried. It terrified him as nothing else did. He has seen the children, ripe with fertility, covered in bulky muscles, and mean. Dangerous.

"As I said, It should be used in small amounts, *only* as medicine, and with someone like me…a nurse…to watch the results and adjust the dosages. A small amount can work miracles, but jumping in for hours and day and being saturated in it for weeks, I can't image the bad effects. Those children would be feral and enraged. Very dangerous."

"Shelly seems so much better."

"I think she is, Marshal Lynn. I treated her with just a little."

"I can see why your people spoke so highly of you and about having a nurse. Thank you. Her husband was killed in the crash, and she's been weak and sickly since."

Helen broke in and asked, "And you've had no sunshine, not any good food, and nothing to nourish your soul, maybe?"

The air marshal nodded.

"Bless you," Bobby said, "I am Robert Paul, actually. Father Robert Paul. I think God sent you to us." Several of his people nodded.

"I don't know. I do know that we are glad you are here with us, for however long you want to stay. Right, Tyrese?" Helen asked. Finding a priest was amazing to her. She thought that even the non-believers could benefit from someone who was loving and kind if this man were like that. "I don't think God is involving Himself here, or someone like Fish would still be with us."

"Indeed," Bobby nodded kindly, "it's nothing we can understand, and I shouldn't have made it seem He was dishing out favors. I suppose we are only thankful for anything good since we've seen only the worst since we crashed here."

"One question?" Scott asked.

"Yes?"

"You were in a plane, a big plane. We heard you were lost, there were searches, and some said maybe you had been hijacked. They couldn't find you. You had to have some beacon, or you were on radar. Why didn't they find you in all this time?"

The air marshal thought, his eyes going a deeper grey. "I've asked that a thousand times. How could they lose a commercial airplane? It makes no sense. Think of yourselves. Didn't people know where you were? Why is no one looking for you? And have you noticed we never see planes over head?"

Alex was glad it was brought up now with everyone in this way. They had asked the same questions earlier.

Stu slapped his knee and said, "I told you. The yellow fog. And then here we are with dinosaurs that died millions of years ago. No one is searching. Doesn't that sound weird? It *isn't* natural. *Something* happened."

No one argued this time.

"So am I right?"

Helen nodded and added, "You may be, Stu. I'm sorry we laughed before."

Stu sat, anger distorting his face. He had known it, but no one believed him until now. It made him furious.

Joe showed the marshal the knife Joy had found, but he had cleaned off the rust, so it was sharp and shiny. "Have you ever seen this?"

"No. We had no knives on the plane."

"Then someone else has also been here or is here. We found this the other day," Tyrese said. "I'd like to explore the beach: walk and walk and see how big this place is. Maybe we'd find more wrecks." He had to add the death of Mrs. Big Brown and say that Mr. Big Brown was still out there.

"I'd like to follow the beach if I could be included with a team that goes," a man named Mick offered.

"We can plan something, right, Marshal?"

"We sure can."

The new people found places to sleep as the others moved around and slept closer together. Kelly felt little as she checked Tom; Joy was right beside him, protectively watching. His stub looked better, and Kelly was convinced the burns almost looked as if they were healing. Kelly left some water for Tom to sip and told Joy to bathe the sore stub with the water before re-bandaging.

"Kelly," Helen hissed, "look at Amanda."

Amanda's back was still charred in places and raw, but Kelly had to remove the stitches since those places looked much better. "How are you?"

"The pain is better. Whatever you're doing, keep it up. It's much less painful. I can lie here and not pray to die now."

Kelly bathed the wounds again and gave Amanda a long drink of the water mixed with coconut water.

Where Amanda lost her fingers, pink skin was forming beautifully. Kelly just shrugged at Helen, amazed and happy.

Pamela swore her face hurt less, Vera said she felt an itch down deep that was like a healing itch, and Jelly promised the stitches could come out the next day if that continued. Durango didn't show a difference.

Shelley was in labor, but it was an easier labor with the pains far apart and only gradually becoming closer. She had more color to her skin.

Alone, Kelly slept well that night. Each time she glanced out of the wreckage, she saw the marshal on guard duty, watching and ready to fight. Jelly stopped checking and slept hard.

Chapter 9: Day Five

Only Scott, Helen, and Alex from the old group went on the trip to explore the beach because the marshal wanted to remain at camp and Tyrese wasn't sure about leaving him alone with their people yet. They liked him, but new people presented new potential problems. Mick, Andrea, and Lilly went along from the new group, so Stu joined them as well.

Far down the beach, they found remains of people and parts of the yacht. They couldn't determine how many people were left, given that most had been eaten by crabs or compys. They took a few pairs of shoes and wadded, dirty clothing they found because it could be washed, and they found pieces of metal that could be used as weapons, but mostly, it looked as if broken furniture had landed at that spot. Broken sofas and chairs had no use right now, but if they wanted them, they knew where they were.

"Did you feel anything before you crashed?"

"Like what?"

Stu thought and said, "I don't know. We were nervous about the storm, but it felt creepy, too."

"The sky was yellow," Lilly said.

"Same for us."

Lilly shrugged and responded, "I felt scared. It looked bad. It's crazy, but I thought about the stories about the Bermuda Triangle."

Stu nodded, "Me, too."

"That's stupid though. I know that's fake."

"Is it? We're here, aren't we?" Stu glowered. He walked ahead.

"Is that...." Helen gripped Scott's hand.

It was an older ship, wrecked on the rocks that split the beach. Although the wood was ruined, it still was there, attesting to the fact that the ship had been well built from very good wood. Someone had had a good sailboat that had crashed and wrecked there; it felt all too familiar.

Puslane grew on some of the rocks, and algae covered the rest. The wood was old and grey from the elements, rotten and worm eaten, and covered in slime and seaweed, but the ship was easy to make out, with the sails long since washed away. The masts were broken and lay in the sand, and the ropes were long gone.

"Is it old?" Andrea asked. She hurried to catch up with Stu, who ignored her.

Alex said he thought the ship had been there a long time, maybe five years or maybe as long as seven or eight.

"I don't see anything we need. If there were anything, it's long gone," Stu said. In a way because the ruins were large, the scene gave him the same feeling he once had when he saw a dinosaur skeleton; he felt awe and curiosity. He didn't think the old bones of monsters were very interesting now that he had seen the real things, alive. It was far different to see hungry creatures than it had been to see dusty bones.

Scott carefully climbed into the husk, soaked by the ocean and was careful to watch his footfalls so he didn't break an ankle. He didn't delve into the darker interior that was littered with rotten beams. Trapped between two heavy boards was what looked like an arm bone, long ago picked clean of flesh. "We're the fossils," he muttered.

If anyone survived this wreck and he couldn't guess, but the violence suggested that no one had, at least not for long. The crash onto the rocks would have felt like crashing a car at seventy to a hundred miles per hour and being tossed around.

"Scott, come on," Helen yelled, "hurry; come see."

He relaxed as he realized they weren't under attack. Crawling out of the wreck, he found Helen waiting, but the rest were down the beach, and he understood where all of them were going and why they were running.

They had been so shocked and interested to see the ship on the rocks that they didn't really look farther down the beach since the wreck was before them and there were no predators. Helen and Scott rushed to catch up.

Far away was a fascinating, but chilling sight.

The beach had been carved away, it seemed. From the water to the tree line was a deep, crude trench, enormous and old. Rocks and sand had been tossed and pushed away violently to make a small bay that the water filled. It could have been strange, but natural except for the sheared off rocks and the huge airliner that sat in the trees. The force of a jetliner had changed the shape of the beach.

They could only see parts even though it was large. The back looked good, old and weathered, but whole. A wing lay toward the back end, left by the force of the crash when it was ripped away from the airplane and burned. What was left was a black mess of warped metal and little else; that it retained a semblance of its shape was surprising. The side, where the wing had been torn, was wide open with sharp metal edges that were wickedly gleaming with a razor sharpness.

Vines grew all over the wreckage. Around the burned wing, the sand was still black, brittle, and melted. Jet fuel had burned hot and brightly there.

A row of seats, filthy and covered in moss and rot, hung sideways, half in and half out of the plane. The seats had long ago lost their fabric but had bits of stuffing with living vegetation all over them. As the group angled around to see, it was clear that the forms in the seats had once been people but were just moss-covered skeletons now. They had died and remained in their seats.

The trees were broken in this area, some uprooted and thrown to the sides. A few were deeply scared and grew in odd ways, and others were burned husks. The airplane had done a lot of damage but took more in response when it hit the thick tree line that held tight.

"I think he tried to land in the damn trees," Mick said.

"Well, he knew he couldn't, so I bet he was hoping for anything. It should have crashed and burned," Alex mused. He didn't understand how this airplane had managed to stay intact.

"We would have, too, but we didn't crash as badly as we should have. Maybe the yellow air cushioned us," Lilly said.

"That's kind of stupid," Stu said, "it can't do that."

"Something saved us, and you have to admit this plane is in better shape than expected," Mick said. He didn't want to fight with Stu, but he frowned, and asked, "How do you know what can do what?"

"Alex, do you think yellow air can make a plane land better?" asked Stu as he laughed.

Alex hated being in the middle, but he shrugged, "I don't know. Stu, you're right that it may be part of this, and we don't know what it does if anything. I agree that it's crazy for this plane or any plane to survive this type of crash, but if there was a storm and the plane wafted in instead of just blazing in, I just don't know."

The belly of the plane was lost in the sand and soil that it pushed to the side and was partially hidden by the ruined trees that the group climbed over, under, or around. The plane, even intact, was terribly battered and bent. Forward of the wings, the plane was twisted at a forty-five degree angle where the trees bent it. The skin of the craft had bent and pulled apart, spilling more seats among the broken trees. The force had tossed people out into the jungle with and without the seats. In fact, as they were thrown, the seat belts had actually cut a few people in half. A pile of very old, brown bones lay scattered, but they were rib cages and skulls; the rest of the corpses were left to rot in the hanging seats.

Andrea tripped over a rib cage and skinned her palms as she caught her fall.

The nose and front section of the plane was smashed, the metal crumpled and rusted, and it looked half the size it should.

"Like our plane," Lilly said, "the front was smushed like this. Everyone was crushed into blobs of bones and blood. Just a steaming pile of flesh that didn't look human anymore...." She remembered their crash, and seeing the random hands or fingers that stuck out of the mess made no sense. She still had nightmares some nights about what she saw when they crashed. Blood had poured from the remains of the plane.

The other wing was gone.

They looked around, but there was no sign of it, and it was clearly torn off the plane, but was nowhere in sight. They searched, but the wing was either deep in the jungle or had just vanished for no reason. Scott whooped when he saw an old sled that hung in tatters. It was from the emergency exit and meant someone had used it to leave the airplane. That meant there had been survivors.

"I wonder how many made it out?" Andrea asked.

"Or if they were injured so baldy they couldn't survive?" Stu muttered. "We just know at least one person came out alive."

"Even if only a small percentage survived, that would mean, what a dozen?" Helen asked. "Where would they go, and what would they do?"

"Wait for help," Alex said, "that's normal. So maybe they camped on the beach."

Unable to get into the plane and seeing no reason to try, they walked back down the sand, wandering around the giant rift that the plane made. After some searching, they found pieces of wood and a few old, broken bits of cups that looked as if it might have been a camp. It could also have been junk that was washed up by the sea.

"I would think this would draw predators. If so, they may have been attacked. If they were, they ran to the trees. Regardless, this wreck is old. Look at the vines. They aren't new ones but thick and gnarled. I'd say this one is twenty years old since the plane style is really outdated."

"I wish we knew the name and details. I bet it's a plane missing from the Bermuda Triangle."

No one said anything to Stu. It was possible.

He yelled and pointed. He had good eyesight because he saw what the rest only visualized as a dark spot on the beach. He was excited and had to be talked into stopping to have a meal and to drink water while they were safe. He wanted to see what was lying all over the sand around the curve of land.

"Let's be sure we are full and hydrated just in case we find trouble. We can use this time," Scott told Stu, "please, wait."

"I've studied this since I was little."

"Studied what?"

"The Triangle. Damn. Are all of you dense? This is it. This is where everyone ends up." Stu finished eating and stood, ignoring everyone who asked him to stay a little longer. He set off alone.

"Tyrese would have set him straight," Scott said. He wished he knew how to lead, but Stu Jones was a wild card. His mind was set.

They finished eating and rested a bit, talking about the airplane and the broken ship back on the rocks. They couldn't disagree with Stu, but nothing made them feel he was right. It was just a tale, an excuse for every missing vessel. It wasn't real. They decided it, but they didn't say it with conviction.

In a little while, they walked down the beach. Scott said that after this, they had to go back. This was their halfway point until they prepared for an overnight venture. If Stu refused to return to camp, he would be left alone. There was nothing else they could do.

As they grew closer, they began to run. It was unbelievable. It was a ship graveyard.

Stu sat on a log, looking at the ships, some small, some larger, some old, and some new that were tangled in metal, wood, and seaweed. He was just looking at all the wreckage with a funny expression.

"Can you believe this? Why? How?" Lilly said, catching her breath.

"They washed up. I think most were wrecks and came ashore but didn't crash like we did. They were already torn apart. Those...the ones that were already wrecks, no one made it. I guess they died in the ocean. Maybe in a storm like ours."

Scott sat next to Stu, and the rest sat on the sand and got drinks out.

"How many are there?" asked Andrea as she looked at the massive wreckage: boats that were battered and twisted into one another, and a mess of ruins that covered the beach and was piled high into the air.

"Five? Six?" Mick suggested.

"I counted at least eight. Maybe ten," Stu told them, "so you see that one? The one that has some red paint? That's the *Saint Christine*. She vanished after she left Beaufort, South Carolina four years ago. That other one? You can see the masts. I think it's the *Dance O' Tropics* that disappeared from the west coast of Florida."

"I'm no expert, but how could they land here? I mean, we're nowhere near there and West Florida? That's a long way," said Mick as he shook his head.

"It was right off Beaufort. I know that for a fact, and you can see as well as I can what her name is. Get closer. There's the *Violet Marie* over there, see? She's blue and a newer craft?"

Lilly's jaw dropped. "I know that boat. Kids talked about it in class…that it vanished. I know because we were planning a senior trip to the beach, and we said we wouldn't get on a boat. It was the second to vanish off the Florida Keys that summer, and that's where we went." She took a breath. "We didn't go on boats, but we went on the trip, and it was on the news constantly. Everyone was looking for it, and it wasn't far off the coast when it vanished or something."

Stu nodded and said, "She was thirty nautical miles off the coast out of Daytona Beach and an expensive, nice boat named after the owner's daughter. John Littleton of the Internet gaming industry owned it. People looked hard for him and his family, but there was nothing. Some said they picked up a storm for a little while, but others said no there wasn't one. It was like the storm was there and then gone within minutes, and it was a huge mystery."

The *Violet Marie* was there. Like the storm, and then, same as that storm, it was gone without a distress call or any word. When she was overdue, the search began, and the mystery started to take shape. Thousands of miles were searched, but there was nothing found: no junk, no wreckage, no survivors. It simply vanished. While the searchers looked everywhere and people worried about the boat of scuba divers, a few days later, the *Havin' a Fling,* a small boat with six people aboard, vanished in almost the same place.

Experts ruled out pirates and thought there had been some water anomaly but couldn't decide what happened. A month later, the search for both was called off, and the occupants were declared dead. Nothing ever washed ashore, and for half a year, people avoided the area when they could.

"I think those are boats that have gone missing in the last five years, some maybe a little longer. One way up there? It looks old. I would say it's been here rotting for twenty or thirty years. There may be a dozen in that wreckage for all I can tell," Stu said.

"I figured you'd be happy to put the pieces together," Helen said. She felt faintly sick at seeing so many boats.

"Naw. I thought I would be, too, but it doesn't feel good. I mean I liked the mystery."

"And this is real. Now you know."

Stu shook his head with a frown and said, "No, not that. It's...don't you see? We are just one of them. One of the missing. They were never found. We won't be, either."

"Does that mean the waters are...I mean is it supernatural? Haunted? Is this like that?" Andrea asked.

Alex had been thinking. "There are wrecks with boats all over the place. It sounds supernatural, but it *is* and *isn't*. We have one thing: a freaky storm comes up and takes planes and boats. It deposits some of them here. We don't know about all, but some, for sure. Do we understand the storm? No. We can call it supernatural and haunted, but it may be something we don't understand. At one time, we didn't understand electricity and penicillin, and you could call both witchcraft."

People nodded.

"Go on," Scott urged.

"We don't understand and never will, I think. Something happens, and the storm grabs airplane and boats. They crash here. Or they crash close and are washed up. I think a few survive. On the other hand, we have an island of dinosaurs. We see no planes searching for us. I think the storm puts some of us in places we don't understand and that are not quite connected to the places we knew before."

"We've already decided that."

Alex sighed and continued, "We decided that, sure. But now we know that Stu is right. It's all related to where we were. People, the legends are right. No one ever is found later. Do you get it? We are one of the many that vanished. This is it. Stu gets it."

Lilly cocked her head and said, "I don't get it.

"We're not going back. There is *no* back. There is here. We're not going to be found. This is home now. The *end*."

Helen felt tears in her eyes.

"They all washed up. Just like we did. If any made it, where are they? Nowhere. The dinosaurs got them," Stu said, angry again. "It isn't bad enough to crash. It isn't bad enough to vanish like the rest, oh, hell, no, we get the fucking dinosaurs as well. Talk about great luck." He tossed a rock at the wrecks.

The rock didn't matter very much, but it thunked a rotten board just as a snort bellowed from the water. Had everyone not watched Stu throw the rock and watched it hit the board, no one would have seen what was swimming towards them.

They were Therizinosaurs, creatures that Alex had only read about a little and considered to be more theoretical than real because they were so unusual in the dinosaur world. These were far smaller than scientists thought: they were only fifteen or twenty feet long and weighed only a ton, except for that, they were as theorized. They could walk on four legs or two, but their forelegs were exceptionally long and tipped with claws like a sloth.

Bluish grey, the animals had pot bellies and loved the ocean and swimming. Omnivorous, they liked to find fruit in the trees but were equally as happy to catch fish and were happy with small prey. They had big teeth that could handle meat or vegetable matter.

There were a dozen of them, and the first two were close to the shore.

"Alex?"

Alex didn't know what to say to Helen, but they only had seconds. If they ran to the trees, the animals would come after them and hunt them down. They were able to climb a little and dig under trees. They couldn't outrun them either. Going into the water was out. There were no choices.

"Go to the wreck. Hide." Alex yelled. He grabbed Lilly and pushed her to run.

The first beast lumbered out and decided his pack would take down the smaller prey since the fishing had been poor that day and they were hungry. The youngest of his pack were very hungry, in fact. The had complained a lot this day. In the creature's memory long ago, he had hunted this area and found prey that smelled like this. Several times. Sometimes the prey had been dead, which was fine, and sometimes they were alive and fresh, which was better.

Those times, the small prey had run and fallen on the sand, but his kind had eaten them. This place had been the site of many successful hunts although sometimes the hunts were years apart. Only once had they found prey a few days apart in this place, scared creatures who huddled and been easy to catch and eat.

Scott and Helen ran full out at the wreckage, not knowing that this was what had befallen the other people who survived the ship wrecks and landed in this spot. The therizinosaurs always hunted here and found those survivors as they waited by the sea for help that didn't come.

Alex dove under a timber as the first creature's head banged into the old wood, snapping boards. It was lucky that there was metal that held him back. Dagger-like claws slashed the air, and Alex crawled in deeper, staying close to the sand and aiming for the heart of the ruins. He saw that Helen and Scott were close, but one of the therizinosaurs came too close because it was smaller and able to get into the debris.

Scott thumped it on the nose and used his spear to stab the animal in the eye.

The air exploded with ferocious squeals and roars as the injured animal retreated, confused and angry. Boards and beams shifted and fell. The snaps of wood breaking was as loud as the screeching of the animals; they were in a frenzy.

One of the larger therizinosaurs smelled blood and fear and jumped on the smaller therizinosaurs, biting at his throat. Another joined in, snapping at the animal's belly. With his eye destroyed, the small creature found itself unable to fight back; his vision was off.

In the wreck, Helen covered her ears.

Scott pulled her to a small cavity that was under an overturned boat. Because the tides had worried at the sand, they were able to find a low place and get into that, hiding like animals in a hole.

At the end of the wreckage far from Scott and Helen, Stu tried to find a hiding place. He felt hot breath on his neck and smelled a fishy, rotten scent that made him feel sick. He tried to get a beam between him and the monster, but the wood snapped easily as a therizinosaurs pushed and clawed, digging at the timber. In seconds, it would have an opening and would snap Stu up and eat him.

Stu didn't plan anything, but Lilly was beside him and was screaming. He meant to stop her from making noise or get her out of his way as he tried to get farther into the wreckage, but as he spun with Lilly in front of him, the therizinosaurs caught her in his claws and yanked. Shocked, Stu stared with his mouth wide open. Lilly was gone in a flash.

As she was pulled out and away from him, her head snapped against a beam, and she was knocked unconscious; her arm was ripped across rusty metal and was almost torn off. Blood spurted in fine droplets as a spray. The therizinosaurs was momentarily distracted by the fight on the beach, aware that his pack members had taken down a weak, injured member and were feeding. Then he went back to his own kill and pulled again. Lilly's arm caught another snag and separated at her shoulder. Her body was taken, but her arm fell to the ground.

Stu took that time to lunge into a small pocket under several beams, skittering away. He saw Andrea staring at him from her own spot on a higher ledge of wood where she squatted, hiding behind what had been the aft of a ship. Her eyes were huge, dark blue, and horrified. She accused Stu with her stare. He wondered what she was thinking; she had to know it was an accident. Maybe.

Stu watched her watching him and then looked at Lilly's arm. Outside the wreck, the therizinosaurs ate her, clawing, ripping, and feeding happily. Only her arm was left. It didn't look like a real arm, but Stu vomited.

Mick climbed around and found Stu, whom he nodded to and then climbed up to Andrea who didn't react, just sat frozen. Mick moved quietly, climbing and staying low so he didn't draw attention.

"Andrea, come on; let's get in a little deeper. This wood won't hold," Mick told her as he pulled at her hand. She didn't look at him, didn't say a word, and didn't move.

The therizinosaurs still tried to get in, but some hadrosaurs were headed to the water as a herd and went still as they heard the battle. They smelled blood and fear on the air. Very carefully, they inched backwards into the trees, but the therizinosaurs saw them and snorted and roared. It would be easier to kill the hadrosaurs in the jungle than to ferret out the prey that hid in the wreckage, and they had already been stabbed and poked in their noses several times.

The leader of the therizinosaurs pack made noises, and his followers dropped their food and ran at the hadrosaurs, chasing them, darting through the trees, undergrowth, and vines, and moving fast along an old trail. It was a long time before the screeches and reverberations of roars faded into the distance.

Alex called, "We need to go back to camp. Now. Let's go; head over to that log, and watch the trees."

He climbed out, wiping away algae and sea weed. He saw what remained of Lilly and shuddered. She was partially eaten and was mostly snapped bones and raw, bloodied flesh. The therizinosaurs was in the same shape. It was disgusting that a human and a monster were left in the same condition as meat to be picked over by crabs, birds, and small dinosaurs. Already compys were coming over to investigate, chittering happily.

Alex didn't have time for the corpses but urged Helen and Scott to hurry. Stu joined them, his face white with shock and fear. Lastly Mick helped Andrea from the wreckage. She was shaking visibly, white as paint, and had no facial expression. Her big eyes stared into space, and she barely reacted to Mick's orders.

At the log, they took only a second for a quick drink of water, grabbed their sled, and began to hurry back. Andrea jogged along when told to and stopped when told to. She was a manikin that moved when given orders.

"Andrea, can you talk to me?" Mick asked when they stopped at the plane wreck.

She didn't say a word.

Mick shook his head and said, "She's in shock. I guess seeing Lilly...they...you know. They were a couple."

"A couple of what? Huh?"

Mick sighed, "A couple. Together."

"Gay?" Stu asked.

"Yeah. Why?"

Stu snorted and rolled his eyes. "Whatever, I guess." He watched Andrea. If she spoke, she would tell that it was his fault Lilly was killed. In fact, it could be said that he used her to save himself. Had he? He wasn't positive. He hadn't planned to move her in front of him, but he had done it, and at some level, didn't he know she would be taken instead? Had she not been there, he would be dead, eaten on the beach.

What if she told? He could deny it, but the suspicion would be there, and then everyone would wonder and think it was possible he had done that. Would they throw him out of camp for murder? Was it murder? Had he killed her? He couldn't think straight.

He didn't want to be tossed away. Andrea, if she told, could cause that. He had found his place, kind of, and Kelly seemed to be on the outs with his brother Tom who was really sick and had only one arm; he couldn't protect Kelly. Stu could. Stu could do a lot that Tom couldn't, and now he was the alpha of the Jones family.

Andrea might make Kelly hate Stu. Just when things were edging his way, she could ruin this; after all, she was an outsider and gay. How unfair was that? Hatred for her surged, along with the shock of causing Lilly's death, and it mixed with the pressure of the last few days, his despair at realizing that there would be no rescue, ever. To top it off, his desire to be the top male and to win Kelly, whom he thought was the top female, made his hormones surge.

While the rest drank water or coconut water, he drank the weird water from the pool that he had poured into his bottle, thinking it would strengthen him. His muscles were slowly building, and he was becoming stronger and more focused on survival. He was entering into an anger he had never known. While he had always been an angry, envious person, he was now becoming more.

"Stu?" Helen asked again. He was staring at Andrea and not responding.

"Huh?"

"I said are you okay? Any injuries? Did you see when she was killed? My God, Andrea watched, I guess."

"Yeah. I saw it. It was horrible," Stu said robotically, "she was ripped apart, but she hit her head, so I think she was knocked out."

"Thank, God. I hope this is temporary for Andrea."

"Yeah," Stu said. What if it wasn't? He would watch her, and if she seemed about to tell, well he would....

He paused. And blinked. What would he do? Was he actually considering killing her; that might be the best.

Stu rubbed his temples as thoughts assaulted him too fast for him to deal with. He wasn't sure what he was thinking. He wouldn't ever intentionally harm anyone. He hoped.

"We need to go faster. I promised to get more purslane for Joe, and it's all over those rocks by the first shipwreck," Helen said as they walked.

Alex said, "I thought therizinosaurs were a fluke, a theory. I never dreamed.... Sue will be amazed. I hate losing Lilly. They were safe in the plane and now look. We're going back after losing *another* person."

"I don't guess we need to keep going out if this is what happens," Scott said.

"Why bother? We know now," Stu added.

"I don't know anything," Alex said, "we know nothing. We only know we are where the ships and planes go. And dinosaurs. Maybe a storm brought them. We know nothing."

No one had anything to add.

They knew nothing.

Chapter 10: Day Five, Evening

Marshal's group was upset over the loss of Lilly and gathered around Andrea, but she didn't react to anyone or anything. She ate when told to but was mechanical. It took a long time to tell all that the group had seen and what they thought. They were divided on theories about the shipwrecks, some saying it was coincidence, and some saying it was a Bermuda Triangle curse.

Alex explained that it didn't matter.

The few things they agreed on were where they needed to stay together, to reinforce the camp, maybe with a line of sharp spears turned outwards around the parameter of camp, and to expect help to rescue them. They had played with the idea and said it was so, but on the evening of day five, for those in a boat wreck, they accepted that they were going to be there forever.

Kelly was surprised when Stu helped her with the patients. He shrugged and said she needed him and smiled, but the smile chilled her. She went along with him and let him help.

Earlier, Shelly's baby was stillborn with the cord wrapped around his neck, and Kelly was unable to save his life. It had been a depressing day, ending with the news about Lilly. Vera was doing better, Amanda was still alive, which was a good surprise, and Tom was hanging on.

"I can bandage him," Joy told Kelly.

"I'm still checking."

"I'm okay, Kelly. You've done enough to me," Tom said dully.

"She saved your life, Tom. Some appreciation?"

Tom glared at his brother and said, "Stu, when you have your arm hacked off and burned, then you can give me advice."

Stu was aware that several were near as Tom lay by the fire next to Joy. Kelly was impressed with his improvement and swore by the water as saving his life. He felt cross with Tom and replied, "It was to save you. Damn. Would you rather be dead?"

"I don't know. I don't know Kelly anymore. I trusted her. You...she...I was betrayed. I said no, and you did this to me." He nodded to his stump. It was less painful, but the memory of the slashing and charring was bright in his mind. He couldn't stop remembering how if felt with every stroke of the machete. He had wanted to die. And then, when it couldn't get worse, it did; they burned him. All of them played a part, but in his mind, he focused on Kelly and hated her. He equated her with the anguish.

"You should have talked it over with him. You could have given him your little mystery pills that Davey the druggie gave you or given him pot to smoke."

"Hey!" Davey glowered at Joy.

"I had to do it fast," replied Kelly but felt unsure now.

"Right. You didn't give him a choice. You didn't give Amanda a choice. Since when do you dish out life and death, Kelly? Don't people get a choice to die if that is their decision? Where's the respect?"

"You'd have let Tom die? You sure are cozy with him to want that," Stu said viciously.

Joy made a face and answered, "I don't want him to die. I'm the only one who thinks people need a choice about being tortured."

Kelly walked away to sit alone. Stu followed her, sitting next to her and patting her back. To his surprise, in a few seconds, she turned and cried against his chest. He held her.

Davey watched and whistled, saying, "Wow. I can't keep up with all this changing.

"I think Kelly is doing the best she can. Can you imagine being in her place and making the choices she has? You should preach less, and think more, Joy."

"Or what? You'll slap me again?"

"Helen slapped Joy?" asked Davey as he leaned in closer. He had dropped his slang but had an urge to add *Dude*.

Joy felt ganged up on and responded, "She did. And for no reason except I told her the truth."

Helen bit back a response.

"I thought you'd be nicer now that you're getting some from Scott."

"That's uncalled for. Mind your business, Joy. Maybe you're mad because Tom is too sick for you to take advantage of him again." As soon as Helen said it, she regretted it and looked at Tom, tilting her head with remorse.

"Whoa," Davey said, "seriously?"

"Helen, enough. Far too far," Tyrese called.

She nodded and walked away with Scott who was slack jawed that Helen had blurted out that information. Now, everyone knew.

"Screw you all," Tom said. He didn't say anything else except in whispers to Joy.

They had to move into the wreck when the troodons came to the edge of the jungle and made noises at them, hooting and roaring. They came down the beach a little way but retreated, unsure of themselves. It was enough to crowd the interior of the broken yacht and have most stand around with spears and clubs.

If that weren't enough to have everyone angry at everyone else and have the troodons threatening them and scaring them witless, another storm came up. It was good to fill the water buckets, and it washed clothing and other items such as sheets and blankets, and bandages that they set out, but the rain pittered and plinked down into the wreck, making many move around or position a can to catch the water so they weren't drenched.

The wind was stronger but not dangerous. It howled and moaned as it whipped through the wreck, making it hard for anyone to sleep. Loud thunder added more noise.

Chapter 11: Day Six

The morning arrived slowly because the storm stayed with a deluging rain, making it chilly and damp. Most, if they slept at all slept an hour and then wrung out water from their covers and clothing and tried to sleep again in another corner. The camp members had used all their strength and power to move the other section over so they made an L shape for places to sleep and for protection. Joe had taught some, Vera in particular, how to weave palm fronds and then coat them in coconut and fish oil, to make them extra water proof, but it was slow going as she learned, and only part was covered and tied to the wreck.

The fronds were over the wreck on the back side, the side that was not against the other wreck and hung over the front, making a cave. Vera slept there as dry and warm as she could be, and beside her was her father Durango; stepmother Connie; and her brother Vaughn. It was the Jones' area.

Stu took Kelly there and tucked her in, even while she sobbed. After a while of his patting her, she fell asleep, and he left to stand in the rain to guard the camp. The last little part of dry space was where Amanda lay because her back had to stay dry, and Helen got a place because she watched over Amanda and rubbed oil and the water into her burns. Scott got a place because he was with Helen.

Tom could stay wet for all Vera cared after she found out he was really with Joy. She had resented Kelly for being smart, pretty, and good hearted, but Vera didn't hate those qualities right now. She disliked Joy because Joy was a whore, and if Tom wanted a whore, he could lie in the damp section.

She would weave again though, and make Connie weave, and they would get the entire place covered because that was her goal.

During the morning, people were coming and going for guard duty, gathering full buckets, and leaving empty ones. There was a real bath tub in the yacht, and they had it, unsure why or what they would do with it, but Davey stoppered it perfectly, and all the fresh water went there. Buckets were dumped into the tub and set back to refill. Anything possible was used to gather water.

"Kelly?"

Kelly followed the air marshal.

He knelt and said, "Look at Andrea's arms. Deep slashes covered them going up and down; she bled out, dead. "How did she get the bruises on her arms?"

"I guess when climbing around to get away from those monster at the wreck."

Kelly thought they looked like bruises from hands. Helen, standing beside her, pointed to bruises around her throat.

"You don't think...did someone do this? No, she did it, right?"

"I don't know. The bruises suggest something else. She was catatonic. Could she possibly have been alert again to do this?

Lynn shrugged and replied, "She couldn't stand losing Lilly."

Kelly and Helen thought of Stanley's dying the same way. Neither said anything but would tell Scott and Tyrese later. And Kelly wanted to tell Stu, making Helen frown.

There was another burial at sea, made only a little better by having Father Robert Paul or "Bobby" officiate.

"We need more of the magic water," Kelly said.

"More? You had a lot."

"I seem to be missing some, and we're low on the beans and Suma root. Could some of you go get more and get back safely?"

Tyrese looked worried and said, "I guess. Who?"

Scott spoke, "Helen and I. We know the way."

"I'm part of your group. I'm the third wheel, and I wanna go," Alex said.

"I'm going this time," Stu announced.

Before the rest could say anything, Kelly replied, "Good, I know you'll keep everyone safe."

Helen, Scott, and Alex traded glances.

"I'm in," Mick said, "we went through hell together, so I'm a part of you guys now."

Scott shook his hand and responded, "Glad to have you." He felt Mick was brave, and with the good food and sunlight, Mick already looked as if he had gained weight, and his skin color was healthy again. He would be a fighter if they were attacked.

"I have no right to ask, but will some more of you go get items out of the plane that will be useful. Joe and I have been modifying the sled with some wheels from the carts that washed up. You can get to the jungle and slide the wheels on, slide on a nut, and twist it tight, and it will roll."

Scott looked at Alex who nodded and told Lynn they would.

"There are another few litters on there. You can drag them back with stuff."

Tyrese asked, "Is there that much?"

"Sure, cushions to sleep on will be wonderful. We brought only a few blankets, but there are pillows. We didn't let Jim take the stuff from the place because if they were to live in caves, we said they could be cave people," the air marshal told them.

Vera was making Connie help with palm fronds, and Pamela was working with Sue, learning how to use the spears and clubs. They were fine with guard duty.

"We may stay overnight. If it's late, we won't chance returning at night. We'll sleep at the plane."

Tyrese and Lynn both nodded.

"You need more help. I wanna go," Davey said.

Harold, Mattie, and Lorie asked to go since they also knew the plane.

"Ga. Ga. Go. Yeah, go." It was one of the first things Durango had said.

"Dad? We're going on a long walk and may be in danger."

"'at's fo me," said Durango, slurring his words as if he had a stroke. Kelly checked him and said the swelling was down and his pupils were small. He followed her finger, stood on one foot, walked

back and forth across the camp, and followed the conversations. He had trouble only as he tried to speak, "I nee to ge up and do sings."

"I don't wanna have to stop and bring you back if you get weird and stop talking or if you get tired. It's a hard walk and overnight," said Stu as he warned him like a parent would a child.

"I ca talkf good now an I ant to be out and do. I ca walkf fine. I talkf. I fi the dinoaos." His slurring bothered him, and he grimaced, frowned, and clenched his eyes shut at times as he spoke.

"My Durango is back!" Connie cheered.

"Okay," Stu said, and then he paused, "okay, Scott? It's your lead, right?"

Scott nodded. Tyrese shrugged, but Scott said, "Not this time."

They left for the trip to the jungle, worried about who would die this time since every trip went badly. Helen spoke quietly to Alex, Scott, and Davey since he was sticking close. Mick leaned in to listen, and Helen sighed; she had meant it for only Alex and Scott.

"Have you noticed that we are still the same...we are us, but we're also changing?"

"Are you getting supernatural now?"

"No, Davey, I need a psychologist for this. The extra is falling away, and we are being refined by this. Like you find a diamond and chop away the rock, and then you cut it and make facets and shine it...it becomes refined."

"We're refined? Fancy." Davey teased her.

She snickered and said, "I think our true selves are showing, and the other had been cut away. Deep down, I am a straight shooter, but I don't say things. I tend to hold back. I say what I think. I've moved past the other. Tom has changed; he is more real and less starry eyed. Davey, you've changed. You don't add *Dude* to every sentence. You don't fake being a druggie nut; you are smart and brave, and you're being that part. You shed the rest."

"Is that good?" Alex asked.

"That's why we need a psychologist. I don't know! For some. But some may not be good at the core when they shed the rest and are refined into whomever they really are." She cut her eyes, and they knew she meant Stu.

"We'll be vigilant and assess each person as he changes. I mean we were wrecked, we found extinct animals, we saw people we cared for slaughtered, we watched Kelly have to do horrible things, and we saw the baby die," Alex said.

Because Andrea had bruises, I think someone killed her. No knife was beside her. And Stanley, same thing."

"Damn," Davey said. Mick breathed out hard.

"What're you talking about?" asked Stu as he walked up to join them. He had been behind, telling Harold and Lorie about the ship wrecks and their histories. Durango supported the idea that they were victims of the Bermuda Triangle, and he had managed to convey his feeling in his slurred words.

"We're talking about our being sorry Andrea killed herself."

"She couldn't stand this new life, I guess. Seeing Lilly die was very bad. She was right with me, and if I had let her go first," Stu paused for effect, "she would be alive. It would have gotten me. I feel so guilty."

"The pool!" Alex again knew no modesty and stripped and dove in, swimming across where he plucked fava beans to eat. He didn't want to talk anymore and felt drained.

"Not much. Kelly says *medicinal* only," Helen warned all of them.

Mattie waded alone in the shallow parts that had flat, rock slabs along the bottom, careful to sit only there or wade. She didn't trust the center of the pond where the others dove a few times.

Helen and Scott went in, Helen blushing again. Davey joined them after a few seconds of embarrassment. Stu dove in, gulping water and eating the beans as fast as he could; he was craving this so badly he was about to jump out of his skin.

Mick dove in, guzzling the water and rubbing it all over his head. Harold and Lorie were a little afraid and began by putting their feet in and testing the water.

"I feel good," Stu announced. He stayed in the water, filling himself with it and filling all the bottles for them, so that chore was finished.

"Thanks, Stu," Helen said.

"No problem, Baby."

Helen looked at Scott and mouthed the word *baby* at him. He gazed with daggers in his eyes and cast a dirty look at Stu. Helen found that after about twenty minutes, her small cuts were healed, and the bigger ones were almost well. Davey told them his sore shoulder was painless. Scott reported the same, and so did Alex.

"My feet were cut from walking, but look, they feel better now," said Lorie as she held a foot out.

Stu caught her foot and said, "Come into the water."

"I'm okay here. It feels wonderful. I feel so strong and healthy."

Davey whispered, "Is it me, or has Stu suddenly beefed up? Look at his flat belly, and his arms are as big as Tyrese's."

Scott nodded and said, "I know. I thought I was imagining it."

Helen smiled and asked, "Can you see my scars from my gall bladder surgery? Only one was big and ugly. Look. Nothing. My God, this water is magic."

"Get in," Stu said as he pulled on Lorie's foot.

"She said no," Harold said, getting angry.

"Are you putting it to her? Huh? Are you her man?" Stu asked.

Harold blushed deep red and shifted his eyes; Stu continued talking, "Nope, she needs a man; Lorie, come play in the water."

"I...I don't swim well. The attention was making her giggle. She didn't get the rising anger and discomfitures.

She slid and squealed softy. Harold grabbed her arm, glaring at Stu.

"I have you," said Stu as he yanked her off the ledge and into his arms in the water. They went under and rose, both laughing.

"You got me all wet."

"Hmmm. Well. Take your clothes off to dry."

"I can't do that."

"Helen is naked. Helen, show us your boobs."

Helen sank lower in the water, close to Scott and blushed. She knew Scott was angry.

They picked beans, dug the Suma root, and packed everything. Harold helped strap items onto the sled but kept looking back at times. Lorie giggled often. Mattie shook her head at Harold.

"None of my business, but what is the relationship with all of you?" Scott asked Mick, Harold, and Mattie, and he looked over to Lorie to include her.

Andrea and Lilly were lovers. Harold was crazy about Lorie, but they had no physical relationship, yet they were close. He had said he loved Lorie, but he said she wasn't ready. Her husband was killed in the crash, suffering for days before dying. Harold explained it very openly.

"Thanks, sorry it's a mess," Scott nodded towards Stu and Lorie who played in the pool.

Lorie spoke, "Mattie was married and was on the plane with her husband Jack and her teenaged son, Jody. When they got home, she was going to file for divorce on the grounds that Jack was sleeping around with every woman he could. If a person had a vagina, he was there, and he had even fooled around with a transgender woman because she had a vagina. That was all it took. He had been sorry every time she caught him and swore to be good, but this was the tenth time, and she was out of forgiveness. Also, this time he didn't swear he'd dump the transgender woman but claimed he loved them both. Lorie shuddered as she told the story.

"Imagine this. I sat with Jody and was livid, just wanting to land and file for divorce, take every penny he had, and make him a pauper with the *she male*," Mattie sighed. And several rows behind, that son of a bitch sat next to his *woman*. His fake woman. I wanted to, scratch her eyes out. But we crashed."

She said she hoped that the crash had killed the transgender slut. She hoped Jack was dead or dying slowly. But neither was injured past cuts and bumps.

"When Jim made his stand, the group was split. Jim demanded to live in the caves and make a life there and to live like cave men; he said he had been on a *Paleo* diet anyway. Jack was all for that, too. They went to check it out and found this pool. Jim said they stayed in it a lot, looked over the caves, and thought."

"The cave is just right up there; it's not a half minute away," said Helen as she pointed.

"They were gone a week…a little group of them. Men and two females. One woman acted normal, her cuts were healed, and she looked stronger and healthier. She was grouchier; that was all. The other female, Jack, Jim, and the others talked about how they were gonna have sex one-third of the day, hunt for food and do cave stuff a third, and then have sex in the pool the other third. They didn't need sleep. It was weird and unlike Jack, even. And they used crude terms. They didn't say have sex but…you know…the F-word….they would F-word all the time and have babies and populate the island."

Helen told her, "That wasn't in the diary. He skipped this part, but there were pages removed."

"I bet he was embarrassed when he got this water out of his head. It affects people differently. Like Kelly said, 'As medicine, it's very good. As a habit, it's bad.' "

"I think like this: it magnifies the personality or doesn't do much but energize. I feel stronger, energized, positive, and...kind of...brave," Alex said.

"I feel that, too. I was embarrassed to be nude in front of everyone, but then I felt fine; I relaxed."

"I feel clear and tough. I feel in charge but not in an angry way. I have more confidence. "

"Me, too. But Stu, he is wilder and more predatory," Davey said, "and Lorie is acting sexy. The hormones are being boosted. I admit sex is on my mind but not like Stu is acting."

Helen bit her lip, remembering that as they swam to the far side earlier and picked beans that hung over like a green tent, they had stopped, and she and Scott had hidden behind the heavy vines and had sex several times. She wanted to go do it again. She knew it was the water and tried to clear her head.

Scott looked at her with need in his eyes.

"What happened, Mattie?" Alex asked.

"Jim and Jack took their group back to populate the world," she told them. "Unfortunately, the transgender woman couldn't have babies, of course. She balked. She didn't like the plans to repopulate the island with humans. She and Jack had a fight that was loud, long, and physical. They traded blows, but everyone stayed out of their argument.

Jack came to Mattie and asked her to join them because she could have babies. She yelled for awhile and refused to go. Had he tried to make her, she would have tried to kill him.

They left, Mattie stayed, but Mattie's son, Jody, went, tempted by the orgies and free sex that was promised; he was a teenager after all. She cried when her son went, wondering how he could leave her but also understanding that his hormones were wild.

"What about the other woman?" Alex asked.

Mattie laughed and said, "We are friends kind of, or rather we have a truce. You *know* her: Shona."

Alex grinned. What a story. A second later, he sobered and realized it wasn't that amusing. "I'm sorry, Mattie. I know that was horrible to lose your husband and then have your son leave that way. You're doing the right thing by getting along with Shona."

"She's pretty cool. I can't blame her. Jack was a smooth talker, and she isn't weird or anything. I mean I said those things and thought bad things, but she is just like any other woman. Normal. I think she felt as cheated as I did."

"You were both smart to stay with the air marshal," Scott said, "just my opinion, but he's a solid guy, isn't he?"

"He's brave and smart and dependable, something my husband wasn't. We think a lot of the marshal. It was the water, but it wasn't. Does that make sense?"

Helen nodded and said, "In moderation. We were in too long today, actually. It's addictive because it makes people feel better. Too much is a very bad thing."

"I think so, too," Mattie said.

"We have to pack some before it gets dark. We were in there for hours, weren't we?" Helen asked.

Scott nodded and answered, "I think so. It makes you stay. The water, I mean."

"When they got to the caves, they realized that, and Jim said to stay out of the pool, for it was only for medicine like Kelly believes.

But the kids sneaked back to it, and then they just wanted to be there all the time. Kids! They stayed in all day and half the night and a six-year-old began to develop breasts and menstruate. They had a lot of sex, and in a short time, they wouldn't leave the pool. Then for some reason they did get out, and they were aggressive and mean. They ran away from all of those at the cave...their parents. All the children. My seventeen-year-old baby Jody led them."

"Oh, Mattie," Helen said.

"I heard he had claimed the six-year-old girl and three other girls as his. It makes me sick. She's a baby! I want to find him and bring him to his senses. I could get to him if I found him."

"It's too dangerous," Harold said, "he's changed, Mattie. We know that."

She nodded absently.

Alex called out that they were leaving, and as they walked away, he looked back and saw that Lorie was nude and that she and

Stu were very busy in the pond. Each time she cried out, Harold shuddered and looked more sad.

Stu and Lorie dressed again and caught up with the others on the trail, and they walked to the plane and surveyed it. Scott made a list of what to take, and they began to load the sled and then load two litters they could drag. The seat cushions, blankets, and pillows would be great. He also wanted the carpet pulled up to take.

"What about the cargo hold?

Harold looked blank, and then his eyes went big.

They had never been into the cargo bay, but Alex knew a way in, there they found bags and suitcases full of clothing, including sock and shoes; medication; and other items that would be useful.

Harold said they had talked about their luggage but didn't know how to get to it from inside the airplane, so they gave up on that idea quickly. He wanted to kick himself for forgetting.

"It's okay. You had a lot going on, and most people don't know about this way to get in. I saw a show on television once...." Scott laughed.

"But we needed all of this," said Mattie as she shook her head and wiped her face of sweat and tears. She felt they had been going through motions and dealing with a lot of drama and had missed what really mattered.

It would take three trips at least to gather all of the items, but they could do it: bypassing the pool except if Kelly needed the beans, Suma, or water. For the first time, they felt a trip out of camp had paid off.

"I want to get into the other airliner and see what it has as cargo," said Alex as he smiled.

"Me, too. I'm in."

Helen laughed and nodded. Mick said he'd like to go as well, and Davey asked to be a part. They would have a strong team, get it done, and find a lot for the camp. They would survive with better things. The random knives, medications, shoes, and crates made this a perfect payoff. Who would have guessed this plane was carrying supplies for a resort; it was like winning the lottery, and it was the first time the group felt lucky.

Fish would have smiled at that and said they were fortunate, indeed.

They kept enough to make comfortable beds in the plane and half of the groups already had favorite places to sleep. Helen slept hard: exhausted from the night before, tired of the drizzling rain, safe in the plane. Should they live here instead? If they did, they would have to walk the trail and go fishing a lot. It would be dangerous. Maybe they should rethink this and move here.

She wondered what Tyrese would think. And she wondered if Alex and Scott would consider it. They were smart.

As she dreamed, she thought, in her dreams, *Stu walked by her, naked, muscular like he was a statue carved to perfection. His body was perfect, but stronger. He moved with grace he had never displayed before.* She tried to wake fully but was so tired that she drifted, instead. In her mind, Stu was there, and then he was gone. Or maybe she dreamed it.

In the morning, she awoke to the plane's door squeaking and saw her dream was somehow real. A very naked Stu Jones fiddled with the door. She asked, "Where were you? I saw you hours and hours ago...maybe eight hours...nine, and you were naked."

"I sleep naked."

"Why are you walking around. Did you go out?" asked Helen who was confused and still sleepy.

"Go back to sleep, Helen," he whispered, "I went out to pee."

"Oh." She saw he was wet. Maybe it had been the rain. That made sense. He was out in the rain and got wet.

"Sleep. Shhhh."

She lay her head back, but something tickled at her brain. Helen opened her eyes wide. He had left eight hours ago and was just retuning. That was why she heard Lorie call for Stu several times in the night because he was gone. He was eating something, too, when he closed the door. Wet fava beans. She didn't dream that; she was awake!

She rolled over against Scott, afraid.

Stu had spent the entire night in the damned pool. Eight hours. She was sure. They had eaten fish and other food Joe packed, but they had not brought any beans up to the plane; they were wrapped and packed, and he didn't go pee and unpack them.

He had been in the pool.

What did that mean?

Chapter 12: Day Seven

They finished the packing and had all they could take. The best stuff, they would come back for; it was heavy but would change their living conditions in wonderful ways. As they packed, Stu disappeared for a while. Because it was still misty and raining a little, Helen couldn't quite accuse him of anything, but he didn't hide it this time. "I went for a bath. All of you should go."

"We have enough," Scott said, but he did think he wanted to go back and make love to Helen in the waters. He took her hand and felt she was wavering. When the sun was right overhead, they stopped and took a long break from packing. Alex suggested a quick trip to the stream, and Mick said a branch was just through a small copse of trees and was deep and clear. They had used that water.

They washed there. Helen scrubbed her hair, hoping to get every drop of the other water off her skin and out of her hair; it made her mind go in peculiar places. She didn't want to behave in bizarre ways. There was nothing they could do as Stu and Lorie went to the other pool.

"It's for medicine only," Helen whispered.

"He's addicted, just like the kids," Mattie said. She looked sad. Harold had a dejected face.

They bathed in the clear water and then ate the rest of what Joe had packed for them, but missing hot, fresh food.

Mick showed them the sea grapes and berries. The best was when Mick found a tree that had a unusual prickly fruit, but the skin was easily removed and fell away as a whole piece, leaving the inside to be enjoyed. The taste was sweet and tart with a creamy, but solid texture. It tasted somewhat like a peach mixed with a pear and lime sherbet. There was a tiny seed deep inside. They ate several and picked them to take back.

"They grow fast. See all the flowers? Those will be little bulbs in a day and a fruit within a few days. They keep growing. We lived on these."

"What do you call them?"

Mick laughed and said, "We called them *peachy tarts*." He laughed.

"I love *peachy tarts*!" said Davey as he ate a fifth one.

"We'll get more when we come back for the good stuff, the miracle crates." Helen smiled.

A faint cry made them pause. It wasn't clear what made the noise. It sounded like a cry of pain. Alex asked how long Stu and Lorie had been gone.

"Over an hour. Two? We need to go back," said Helen as she gritted her teeth, "I'll get them."

Alex nodded but said he would go along. He had a bad feeling. And they still had to watch for dinosaur attacks. It could happen.

At the pool, neither Helen nor Alex understood exactly what they were seeing. But it seemed to be something terrible. Lorie was on her back on rocks right above the pool; it was a small ledge that almost touched the water but was covered when they were in the water because it was so low.

All around Lorie was blood. It dripped into the cloudy blue-white water. Her lower half was bleeding. When she twisted, they saw her back was scraped and her mouth was bleeding. So was her nose. Had something hurt her and Stu was there trying to help? She cried and moaned, "No. No. *NO!*"

Alex ran because he understood before Helen did. He had a spear and a big club for protection from the dinosaurs. He dropped the spear, afraid he would use it. Leaping into the water from the edge, he slammed the club against Stu's head. Stu went rigid and fell back into the water. Alex dragged him to the side and dropped him.

Helen was shocked. Why had Alex hit Stu? What was wrong with Lorie? She ran to her, and her jaw dropped. She wasn't sure, but Lorie seemed to be saying no. Helen didn't know if this were the result of a consensual rampage of sex, or if she said had said no and Stu still raped her; whatever the reason, her female parts were gushing blood. Helen pushed her into the water and jumped in to keep her from drowning. Maybe the water would help her wounds.

Helen shivered, wondering what it took to do the damage she saw between Lorie's legs. How had this happened?

"What's going on?" Scott asked. Mick, Mattie, Harold, and Davey followed.

"My, God," Mattie cringed as she saw the bloody water. "What happened? What happened to Stu?"

"I don't know. She looks as if she were beaten and raped almost to death. I hope the water can help her. As for him…."

"I hit his ass with a club. I knocked him out," Alex said, "he didn't even act as if he saw us and was…he kept…he was still…he wouldn't stop…."

Scott kicked Stu in the ribs.

Startled, Stu woke and sat up, grabbing his ribs and then grabbing his head where a nice lump had formed over an ear. "What the hell?"

"You tell us. What were you doing to Lorie? She was bleeding and begging you to stop."

"Huh? She…we were…."

"No, you *were*. Stu, she is bleeding badly and torn up. You must have…." Scott was at a loss for words. He glanced down and felt his legs go numb and ice fill his veins. No. He prayed it wasn't real. Tears stung his eyes, and he felt a rage building. Without a word, Scott spun and hit Stu in the jaw and stomach quickly. Stu might have been getting stronger and leaner, but Scott was, as well, maybe only through hard work and not water with steroids; he was just as tough.

Stu swung; Scott ducked, and then he pounded Stu again in the face. Stu fell, but Scott kept going. With a knee across Stu's stomach, he slammed his fists into Stu's face over and over. Blood poured. Before he knew it, he had Stu's head and was slamming it on the ground. Davey ran and tackled Scott, knocking him away.

"Scott, Scott, you're killing him. Stop it. What is it? You have to stop and talk."

Scott sat back. He saw the mess he had made of another man's face in his absolute rage. Helen slowly walked out of the water, pulling Lorie and put her on the rocks. "We need to dig a grave," she said simply.

"No, no, she's? Is she? How? What happened to her? He raped her? How did that kill her?" Harold wailed and paced around the area. Mattie crouched and cried.

Lorie was on the rock, and Helen sat beside her, drying off. Mick went to get a blanket from the sleds, and he carefully wrapped Lorie. "We'll take her back and send her to the sea. Like the rest. I don't want anything getting to her. Helen, Scott, we don't understand really what happened."

Helen shook her head and said, "She was all torn up, but even rape, I don't know what happened. Scott?"

Alex found the item Scott had already seen, but everyone else had overlooked it because they were looking at Scott, Lorie's body, or Stu. It was the club that Stu carried in case he were attacked. This time it seemed he had hit Lorie in the mouth and nose, beat her, raped her, and then used the club as a sexual sadistic device of torture. After that, he raped her again. But the club was so big and rough that it must have torn up her insides, making her hemorrhage. Her neck and stomach were chewed. Not just bitten, but there were pieces ripped and torn away, leaving livid tooth marks.

Alex stopped, walked over to the side, and vomited. Mick grabbed Harold as Harold lunged for Stu to hit him again. The man was just coming around, and he face looked like raw hamburger meat. Alex took the bloody club and threw it at Stu, hitting him on the shoulder.

Scott motioned them to come with him.

They added Lorie's body to the sleds, making them heavier, so they had to leave one behind. Scott didn't care. They pulled them along the trail and didn't talk. There wasn't anything to say.

Davey wondered if Stu would follow them, or if he'd go away, or if a dinosaur would find him and eat him. Would he get in the pool again? He had so many questions, but none that anyone could answer. He felt dejected. For once, no creatures attacked the group out exploring, but Stu had to ruin everything, so they were going back to tell everyone that another person was dead.

As for Stu, Davey didn't know what they would say. They had to wait.

Chapter 13: Day Eight Evening

That evening they lowered Shelly, her baby, and Lorie into the sea. Shelly had not recovered from having her child. Kelly said it was as if Shelly's heart just stopped because she didn't want to go on.

The mood was up and down. This also meant the water wasn't a miracle cure-all but only a tool, like a needle and thread, or antibiotic cream, or a bandage. It didn't ensure anything. It certainly didn't save Shelly and her baby; Kelly felt cheated by this turn of events, but she could give up or learn from this, and do better next time.

How foolish she had been to believe in magic. It was only a natural pool of concentrated substances, and *there were no magic, no gold, and no unicorn;* she giggled a little to herself with that thought. *Silly Kelly.* But Tom, as mean and mad as he was and snotty old Joy couldn't take away what Kelly believed in and trusted. She would heal everyone she could, no matter what it took. She would not allow respected suicide. Nope. Before she would have allowed it, she would have nodded and thought each person should decide his own terms of life and death, same as a book she read once about some stupid zombies. But the main character believed in respect of choices.

Kelly did, too.

Right before she sat down and motioned for Joe to lay a red hot blade against Amanda's back, she saw the char, heard the screams, and smelled the stink of burned flesh that baptized her into a new line of thinking. She would save everyone. Period, like it or not because she needed them and because after all this, they didn't have the right to die. They had the responsibility, no matter how agonizing, to live.

She had changed.

People were angry with Stu; sad about Lorie, Shelly and her child; excited about the cargo that would be brought; happy with what the team managed to get back; confused over what had happened; and worried about what else might happen. The emotions were flittering all around, and there were tears at the same time as there were laughter and whispered uncertainties.

Joe calmed them and said, "Stop. All of you are guessing and feeling down, but you are living another day, something many wish they had. Don't insult their memories. Look what I have."

"What is it?" Kelly smiled, trying to get the others to look and see.

A huge pan of coconut breaded shrimp, and that wasn't easy to manage, and I have a sweet, hot dipping sauce, I do. There is my version of scampi with oil, garlic, and a little wine. Those shrimp are happy fellows. The squid is marinated with canned tomatoes, so sorry they aren't fresh, and some Mexican seasonings, peppers, and wild onions. Canned beans. It's a sort of stew, but you eat it on this flat bread I baked for it, okay?"

"That's wonderful, Joe."

"Hey, I love squid," Davey said.

"The other steaks that we didn't smoke I wrapped with fat, thick fat, and purslane, and wild onions, and beside the steaks is sort of a salad made of the palm hearts, canned green peas, canned mushrooms, carrots, and some shrimp, in a ginger white sauce that is thick, and oh, so delicious. I outdid myself."

"It's like a fancy restaurant, Joe. Amazing. How can you do this?"

"I can't when we are out of canned vegetable, but you said you found crates of them?"

Scott laughed and said, "A hundred times what we scavenged here."

"Then, with the fish, all kinds of fish, we'll eat like kings. And we're going to trap those compys and fix them like chicken, stuffing and all, fry them, bake them with veggies, and keep eating. Now what do you wanna stop there for, Davey? Try a bite of each dish."

Davey grinned and replied, "I don't mind if I do." Alex, Scott, and Helen motioned the others to come eat which they did, complimenting Joe over and over.

Bobby said, "The Lord provides the fish, the fruit, the vegetation, the foodstuffs, and a good cook. We are thankful that this is tasty, hot food and that we're not in a desert. Feed the belly well; feed the soul. Amen, let's eat."

The mood was better after that little prayer, and everyone eagerly filled plates and ate hearty.

"You rock, Joe," Mick called.

Marshal Lynn laughed quietly and added, "I'll gain the weight I lost. Cheers to our cook."

Joe smiled and blushed.

After their delicious meal and while relaxing, they were lax in guard duty; they jumped up in alarm as a figure darted through the trees. It was smaller than the troodons, but it broke through and came towards them. The weather was misty, and when the lightning lit the sky, they saw black clouds boiling in. Between the thunder and rising wind, they nervously watched the strange, hunched figure.

Spears ready, they waited.

"Stu," Durango called out.

It was him. He was pulling the litter they had to leave, a heavy litter, but he kept his head down and used his strength to bring it with him. When he was at camp, the spears remained upright, but he set the litter down with all of the bundles in view and sat down on the sand and drank from his bottle. It was plain water. He showed them it was clear.

"Yeah, I washed my face in the pool, and it helped. I used the pool," he said, "I drank and ate from it, or I'd not be here now. I would be back there and dead."

"You have a lot of nerve returning here," Lynn said.

Tyrese added, "You aren't welcome anymore. Why would you dare return?"

Stu shook his head. "Scott is one bad ass fighter. I'll give you that, but I could have taken him. Think. The reason I didn't was that I couldn't. Kelly, look at my back. Please. Just do that one thing, and then I *think* we can discuss this."

"We're not discussing. You're leaving," Tyrese said.

Kelly scowled but walked to Stu, knowing if he touched her, the rest would skewer him. His face looked rough, but she could tell the water had helped. He and the water did well; it worked on him better than it would most. That was his misfortune, too, from what she heard.

Using the fire light when Stu turned, Kelly saw stab wounds. Several were very deep. Had the water not helped him and sealed some of the injuries, he would have bled to death from any one of the wounds. She moved back and looked at the rest and said, "Water helped him some. As it is, he needs stitches and maybe cauterizing."

"He did it to himself," Mattie yelled.

"He couldn't have stabbed himself in those places at these angles."

"Helen, when you ran to me about Lorie, was there a lot of blood?" Stu asked.

Helen nodded. "Yes, she was bleeding badly."

"In the water?

Helen thought, *There was a lot of blood, but things had happened so fast.* "Yes, the water was pink," she replied.

"What did you see?"

"I saw her torn up. I saw you between her legs...."

"Doing what?" his voice had no anger but was only tired.

"You were there naked."

"Was I doing something? Was I moving?"

Helen closed her eyes. What did she see, and why did it matter after what he did to Lorie? "She was crying and saying no. You were between her legs and your hands were down there. You were between her legs, Stu."

"Did you see my dick?" He had to be blunt.

"Yes!"

"Then how was I raping her? You saw my hands splashing water up to where she was hurt. I didn't do anything to her."

Alex moved closer, ready to kill Stu right then. "Who did? Lie. Lie so I can stab you in the heart."

Kelly held out a hand and added, "He has stab wounds. There has to be more to this. Hang on."

"Three kids. Wild. Tan, filthy, long hair with feathers and spears, and one had a knife. They said it was their pool. I got that much, and then one said they should kill us and take us back. Do you know what the other said?" Stu laughed almost hysterically, wiping his face, and he repeated, '*Yeah, good eatin'*.'"

I popped one in the head, but he was thick skulled and didn't budge. The other landed on my back; he had circled us, and he came at me, stabbing like a manic. I couldn't get him off me. When I hit the pool, he stopped and climbed out, sure I would drown or bleed out. I was on the edge and lay there. I guess I looked dead, and he figured I was dying."

"Kids?" asked Lynn as he cocked his head.

"Wild ones. Savages. I saw them hit Lorie in the face a few times, and then they took the bat I dropped, and oh shit, they hurt her. She was unconscious, but they did it. They...they didn't just bite her. They tore off parts and ate them. They ate at her."

"My, God," Helen whispered.

"One said they should leave in case a bunch of us were around. The other laughed and said they would ask Joey? Joe? Someone about coming for all of us."

"Jody," Mattie said, her face ashen.

"Yeah, Jody."

Mattie looked up and responded, "He didn't know that is my son's name. I told the rest, but he wasn't there to hear the story."

Alex lowered the spear and said, "Get him some rum or whatever we have."

Alcohol was another item that had survived the wreck, the best alcohol, and they had a lot, but Kelly had claimed it for medicine, days before. Joy brought the bottle and a cup. Stu drank some and sighed.

"Get my stuff. He needs to be stitched and cleaned," Kelly ordered.

"You saw me between her legs, but I was trying to save her. I was bleeding like a stuck pig, Helen. And Scott, didn't you wonder why I couldn't fight back and just ended up taking the beating of my life?"

"I guess," Scott wasn't convinced, but he felt there was a strong possibility he had made a mistake.

"Two more things: one kid had a weird birthmark on his cheek. I saw that. It was like a half moon and dark red."

"Port wine birthmark...Ricky. I knew him. He is...was...he was with us before all of that," Mick paced and said, "Stu can't have known about Jody and Ricky unless they were there. He described them perfectly...how they dress. He was stabbed. Did we make a mistake?"

Stu took a deep, painful breath and replied, "Yeah, a big one. I *didn't* kill Lorie. *They* did and almost killed *me*. And you came close to finishing me. The pool does heal, but it is dangerous, too. It kept me alive, and I got out and brought the stuff on the sled. I am stronger than ever, but the knife, it doesn't care; it takes blood," he said as he hissed as Kelly cleaned his wounds.

"You said two things," Scott said.

"Oh, the one boy, he carried a staff. On it carefully tied was a human skull. They hunt people. He was the one who did that to Lorie. Ate parts of her."

Mattie's jaw dropped. "What? What are you saying?"

Marshal Lynn put a hand on her shoulder and said, "You didn't listen carefully to Stu. The children. They are cannibals, Mattie. They hunt *people*. They will be hunting *us*."

The rain began to pour in sheets, and everyone scattered. Kelly helped Stu to the wreckage that was better than ever because of Vera's work on palm fronds.

Scott reached out and caught Stu as he stumbled.

Stu looked at him blankly. "Oh."

"I screwed up; I'm sorry. I can't say anything else except that I believed in my heart it was the right reaction. I made a mistake."

Helen, looking tired, said, "I don't know what to say. I'm sorry."

"Me, too," Stu said.

"I don't know how to make it better," Helen said. Alex put an arm around her and nodded. He felt badly.

Stu was about to collapse and was trying to get where Kelly wanted him so she could work. Poor Kelly, always stitching and trying to save people even if they didn't want it.

Tom had been resting and got the news from Joy, both the *before* story and the *after* story. He sighed and said, "Stu, always a mess. He can't get anything right."

"I still don't trust him," Joy whispered.

"Good. Don't. Even if that's true, he's done bad things. I can feel it. Badness is rolling off him; you can almost see it."

"Some are whispering that they believe him but think he was abusing Lorie before, maybe...." Tom stopped talking as Kelly settled Stu close by in the medical area on the bottom deck.

As Stu took another long gulp of rum, he lay on the bed so Kelly could work, using the candle she had as light. It was fine because in one bundle were more candles. Everyone would be pleased to see what he dragged back. He had told the truth. Most of it. What people suspected was true. Lorie was sexed out, and he wasn't. He forced her. He guessed it was rape, but what did that matter since he had also murdered that girl, Lilly, by pulling her in front of him. And there was the other one, Andrea. She had to die before her story was told and caused him trouble.

And there had been the paralyzed boy that was too far gone to save and needed a merciful angel that could release him. Amanda and Durango, Tom and Vera, they had come close to being released.

Sure, he was an accidental killer, and he was a murderer, and he was an angel of death, but he didn't mean to be those things. He just was. Someone had to be strong. Someone had to survive. They needed him. Even if they didn't understand, they needed him, and he had to do whatever it took to be there.

He didn't quite know about his actions with Lorie. They were cloudy in his head.

Scott was still saying he didn't know what to say or do, and Helen was saying she was worried about the savage children.

Tyrese repeated Helen, "I don't know what to do to make this better."

Stu raised his head, managed a chuckle, and said, "Oh, I do. I'll lead this one. Before they come to get us and eat us, bastard cannibals, we're going to do what you said, Tyrese. As soon as I am okay, we are going for them."

"Yeah," Tyrese and Marshal Lynn said it at the same time, "all of them."

Stu grinned and said, "We're gonna clean all out of them. We're going hunting for cannibals. Hey, damn, Kelly, that hurts!" He began to squirm and yelp.

"We'll get them, Stu," Scott said. He couldn't think of what else to say to fix this.

Stu raised his voice as Kelly cleaned and stitched and yelled, "Gonna kill them all for Lorie!"

Chapter 14: Day Twelve

In the four days after the trip to the plane and the loss of Lorie, teams went back and forth without incident and brought back the crates and bundles from the cargo hold, cheering everyone. They had everything the resort had asked to be shipped. There were sheets and blankets, and shower curtains, dishes and cooking utensils, a whole box of randomly sharpened knives, boxes and boxes of candles, cleaning supplies, tarps, towels by the hundreds, bags of personal hygiene items, and even medical kits, along with crisp white napkins that Kelly immediately claimed for medical purposes. The resort needed all of those items to restock.

They didn't need the other things the teams found such as electrical appliances or anything else electrical.

But one of the two best things they found and brought back was something the resort manager had ordered for guests to learn to play: archery sets. Marshal Lynn was thrilled. All that time, the sets had been underneath them. It made Lynn embarrassed and angry, but also glad. Had they found it sooner, Jim and the kids would have taken more than half to the caves.

Alex was designated as a hero.

The other best thing they found were crates of liquor and food: dried beans, rice, canned vegetables, tinned meats, seasonings, and random other foods that the resort needed. Joe said that with fish and an occasional dinosaur, they could live three years on this food.

Alex said maybe there would be more in the old airplane when they had time to go and look into the hold. He looked forward to that.

Vera walked around with a limp, Durango talked more and worked at learning to speak more clearly, and while his spirit was lessened, he was good as a guard. Vera liked to stand guard with him, and she practiced with the bow and arrows every day, determined to learn to be a great guard and an archer, like some ancient super hero.

Tom didn't talk to Kelly except when he had to; otherwise, he stayed close to Joy. Slowly, he began to walk around and try to do things with his one arm. Though he was often frustrated, he kept trying. He didn't forgive what was done to him and blamed Kelly in full, but he *did* want to live.

Amanda was still in bad shape, so Kelly wrapped Amanda's body like a mummy, and despite the pain, Kelly had her try to stretch to keep mobility.

The creatures were staying away although sometimes they saw flashes of Big Brown wandering through the trees and looking out at the beach to the humans. He hadn't come close yet, but he stalked them. His presence kept the troodons away, so it was a trade-off.

It was a few days later that a storm boiled up during the day, and it looked just like the one the survivors had seen, both those on the yacht and those in the airplane. Clouds turned deep purple, the air became yellow as urine and smelled just as bitter and briny, and the waves came in tall and fast, breaking on the rocks.

All dug quickly in the sand, digging with their hands or using the tools they had found in the crates. They dug hard and for a long time. They hoped the trench and the piled up trees would keep the wreckage section of their yacht-home safe. They worried.

Most of the big waves broke way down the beach where they could see them, but where they felt it was far safer.

Thunder echoed and exploded, lightning split the sky, making the black and purple clouds show their fury, and rain fell hard, battering the survivors who hid in the wreckage. They stayed partially dry, but mostly only wished it away.

In a little while, everything was quieter: the wind settled, and the rain stopped; all the buckets were full of the fresh water and were running over.

"What's that?"

Alex stared hard, willing himself to see more clearly, "Is it...is that a ship?"

"A yacht smaller than ours," Stu said. He was irritated that the storm and his injuries kept him from being out there looking for the sons of bitches who killed Lorie. Cannibals.

"It's intact."

"It's on its side," Stu corrected Alex, "and look at that wave. Think we came in on one like it?"

The wave was dark and large. If it hit the wreck, they'd all be swept away, lose everything, and probably die. Helen had handed out all the life jackets to as many as would take them.

She watched.

It angled away from them. It wouldn't crash on them thankfully, but it carried the boat high and moved fast.

"There it goes," Stu called.

The wave ran out of room and had already risen all it could, so it hit the rocks and sand and crashed, dashing away its power and fury. The yacht slammed onto the rocks and beach like a tossed toy.

The group watched.

In a few minutes, they saw the upper half of a man's bloody body, and he rolled to his back, seemingly unaware of the other wreck and of those who watched. The man yelled loudly to the people who were in the wreckage, loud enough that everyone could hear him, "Just hang on. Help will be here soon. Wait for the ambulances."

Vera snickered.

"Oh, my dear, God. It's got to be a coincidence, right? Is it just a weird coincidence, Stu? Tell me that isn't *her.*"

Stu frowned, wondering what in the hell was wrong with Scott. *Her* who? What was a *her*? He saw only a newer, sleek craft, a smaller yacht that was a pretty shade of blue, and was that a name? The boat had a name, of course.

Stu blinked.

"Coincidence?" Scott asked, "because it isn't possible at all. There's a reasonable answer, right?"

In a daze, Stu began walking over to the yacht, his face pale and far more terrified than he had ever looked before. No dinosaur had caused this type of sheer horror on his face.

A few followed him: Alex, Helen, Tyrese, Tom, Mick, Kelly, and Davey.

"Oh thank, God. You're here to help? We're wrecked; we...." The bloody man sat up on the sand, his head and arm bleeding badly.

"Who are you?

"I'm John Littleton. I own this boat...."

"Where did you come from?"

"Florida. Dayton Beach. Look, we need help...."

Stu still stared like a white wax figure and asked, "What's the date?"

Littleton told them; he was five years off on his date.

"He's hit his head," Kelly said.

"No. What's your boat's name?" Stu asked, but they could see the first part of the name right above the torn metal, and the second name was partially legible. Stu needed to hear it.

Alex gulped. Scott grabbed Helen's hand.

Mick began breathing hard, almost hyperventilating and said, "Coincidence. *Please*."

A yacht that vanished five years before and that now was lying, in the graveyard of boats down the beach had the same name, was from the same place, was lost on the date the man said, and was owned by John Littleton. It was the same one.

"The name?" Stu asked again. His head began to spin. "The name, the name, the name. What is the damned name?"

The man leaned away in fear and answered, scared of these strange people. He told them, "It's my boat, named after my daughter."

"Yeah," Stu urged, "*I know*."

"It's the *Violet Marie* ."

Chapter 15: Again, and Again, and Again.

"What does it mean?" Helen asked.

Stu swallowed hard and said, "I think in five years, give or take a few years since we don't know…." He stopped an hysterical laugh from boiling up and out. Everyone looked at him with sheer terror, "I guess we're gonna wash up here again, and so it will all begin again…."

"All of us? The same?" asked Alex as he thought hard.

"Or maybe those who died, I dunno; won't we have stories to tell ourselves? Avoid the troodons that will rush from the trees and come rip you apart or the others, I dunno. We have to do it all again, and it's another us…." Stu faded to laughing so hard he sat down and pounded at the sand.

"*Violet Marie,*" Alex muttered, "again. Time loop. The dinos went extinct and came back. How do we know this is our first time?" Alex demanded. What if this is the second or tenth or fiftieth time we've looped?"

"Stop," said Kelly as she knelt and checked the man. He was confused, "stop saying that."

Stu lay back and laughed harder, scaring everyone, but Alex could identify. He felt as if he were going mad, as well. "I could be Alex 2 or 3."

"Stop!" Kelly screamed, "just stop. All of you are going nuts. So stop, and help me."

The man had a hand over a badly bleeding gash on his arm, and blood was staining the sand. "There are others; they need help. I feel...I feel like I'm dying."

Stu sat up, sobered, and leaned forward, his eyes dark and wicked-looking. He was more afraid than he had ever been, and his heart could barely stand its own uncontrolled, thumping pace. Stu's voice was quiet, making his response far more bloodcurdling. He told the man and those around, "Don't worry if you die. See on Extinction Island, you come back. Over and over and over."

"Huh?"

"You'll see. Welcome to hell."

(Fort Worth: 2014)